and other stories

TO:
Tammy,
with Best wishes.
Eyen Dave
08/11/23
2nd book in this series.

Love in Tuscany
by
Upen Dave

TO:
with Best wishes.

# THE GOLD DIGGER AND OTHER STORIES

## Upen Dave

Kindle Direct Publishing

Editing: Rebecca Grubb @ www.sterlingwords.com
Formatting: Anessa Books @ www.anessabooks.com
Cover design: Karen Phillips @ www.phillipscovers.com

For Dad

# CONTENTS

# THE GOLD DIGGER

As soon as Vic pulled his red, two-seater Mercedes convertible into the Wine Bistro restaurant's parking lot, he purposely revved the engine. The deafening *vroom...vroom* caused everyone in his wine-tasting group to turn their heads in his direction. They were sitting on the restaurant's open porch and had already begun sipping wine. The twenty-member group was enjoying a beautiful June evening in Columbus.

"Here comes Vic the Gold Digger," someone quipped. Everyone laughed. Nadia, a new member, immediately turned around to assess this "Gold Digger". She noted that Vic was a nice-looking man in his early forties. He was tall and masculine, with thick black hair, a handlebar mustache and a Mediterranean tan.

He walked straight to the bar, greeting everyone in his path. He poured himself a Merlot and raised his glass towards the group saying, "Cheers!"

This was the first meeting for Nadia, who had recently moved from Michigan to the Buckeye State. She was a stunning thirty-something: petite, well-dressed, with flowing golden curls and flawless ivory skin. Vic strolled over to Peter, the group's organizer. "Say, who is the new beauty over there?"

Peter gave him a knowing smile and answered, "Nadia just moved here from Michigan."

Vic continued talking to a few old friends, but after a few minutes, he strode up to Nadia and introduced himself, "Hi. I'm Vic. Welcome to our wine-tasting club."

With a charming smile, she replied, "Hello. Nice to meet you. I'm Nadia."

After taking a few sips of the wine of the month, Vic returned to the conversation. "Are you a local? I haven't seen you until today."

Before answering his question, Nadia glanced around at all the Buckeye T-shirts and hats. She tried to subtly tuck her Michigan State keychain into her purse. "Well, I hope you don't kick me out of the wine-tasting club for this... I moved here from Michigan." There was no love lost between the two states, thanks to an intense college football rivalry.

"Around here we don't utter that state's name. I hope you understand," Vic said, sounding like he was only half-joking. . He held up his right hand and pointed to his palm. "Show me where you lived." It seemed like an odd gesture, but anyone who has ever visited Michigan knows the "mitten". If you hold up your right hand it forms the outline of Michigan, with your thumb as the peninsula.

Smiling broadly, Nadia placed her finger on the makeshift state map to show her previous location. Vic closed his palm over her finger and gently held it. "Oh, I guess we'll let you stay. So, what brought you to Ohio?"

Slowly extracting her finger from his grasp, she responded, "My job as a fashion designer for the Victoria Secret division of the L Brands Company." *And I hope it won't keep me here long. I might murder people come football season.*

He looked at her shapely, fashionably-dressed figure and commented, "Designer? I would have guessed model."

She blushed and quickly changed the subject. "And what's your occupation?"

He gave her a wink. "Full-time engineer and part-time gold digger."

Nadia's eyes widened. "In that case, you're hitting on the wrong girl. I'm not a rich woman."

Vic laughed loudly, exposing his perfect white teeth, "I'm not that type of gold digger!"

Before he could provide further explanation, Peter announced, "Ladies and gentlemen, may I have your attention, please. Tonight's contest for the best Merlot will now begin."

When the wine tasting was finished and most of the group were leaving, Vic suggested that the party continue at his house, which was nearby. Some, including Nadia, agreed to join him. He encouraged them to explore while he opened a few more bottles. Guests wandered across the marble floors, admiring the oil paintings on the walls. A well-groomed English shepherd trotted around among them, sniffing, before settling in the corner.

After a few minutes, the guests had spontaneously collected in front of a glass case in the front hall. The handles, feet, and hinges were beautiful metalwork, and the corners of the glass were etched with scrolls and flourishes. Even though it was beautiful, it was clear that it was designed to keep its contents safe. The glass was thick and the frame was steel. The shelves were crowded with a wide variety of valuables, which glittered under the cabinet interior lights.

The case held a stack of gold bars, a pile of silver coins, sparkling jewelry, an antique-looking silver tea set, and many objects whose labels revealed that were extremely rare: arrowheads, relics from the Civil War, even a meteorite. The centerpiece of the display, resting on a rich velvet jewelry box, was an eighteen-karat gold necklace with a huge diamond pendant. The label stated it held one hundred diamonds, and the matching earrings each held twenty. Nadia's mouth fell open when she saw them. She simply could not look away.

"I knew I would find you guys here!" Vic had appeared with a tray of stemware and uncorked bottles and began pouring for his guests. "Well, what do you think of my treasures?"

Nadia was mesmerized by the gold necklace and the wheels started turning in her beautiful head.

Someone asked Vic how he found all the artifacts. "When I go to the beach, lake or ocean, I take my Garrett metal detector. It detects items on land or underwater and changes pitch to differentiate between junk and valuable metals. It will tell me the type of metal and its depth. Based on that information, I'll use my scoop and dig up the object. This is a professional piece of equipment, not the twenty-nine dollar toy metal detectors you see people with on Florida beaches."

The dog came over and nuzzled his owner's free hand. "Hey, Titan," Vic said. He took a sip of his wine and savored it. "Seven generations ago, one of my ancestors went to California during the gold rush of 1849. He worked hard and made some good money. So you see, 'gold digging' is in my blood."

Everyone was impressed by the collection, and after admiring it for several minutes, Vic led them away to show them the patio and fire pit. But Nadia just stood there gazing at the case. She couldn't take her eyes off the necklace and earrings.

"Aren't they magnificent?" Peter had walked up behind Nadia.

She reacted, without pausing. "Oh yes. Very elegant!"

His next question took her totally by surprise. "Would you like to have them?"

Nadia looked at him quizzically. "What?"

He leaned closer and whispered in a conspiratorial tone, "There are only two ways that you can take possession of them. Either marry Vic or steal them." With that pronouncement done, he left the room.

The impromptu party lasted until midnight with more wine, music, and dancing on the patio.

Nadia left with the crowd, but then drove around for half an hour, circling back to Vic's house. The driveway was empty, but she could see that there were still a few lights on inside the house. *Good, he's still awake.* She checked her makeup in the rearview mirror, then took a deep breath and got out of the car. She walked steadily up to the door and rang the bell. Seconds later, the door swung open. Vic looked confused but happy to see her.

"I'm so sorry to bother you, but I left my purse on the dining room table."

"Oh yes, please come in. I'll get it for you." While Vic found her purse, Nadia waited in front of the glass case, gazing at the necklace set. She heard him approach.

"Will you turn the living room lights down?" she asked, still staring at the case as he handed her the purse. "The lights inside the case make that necklace sparkle so beautifully."

"Only a fool would turn down an opportunity to stand in a dark room with a beautiful woman," he joked. But Nadia had other plans.

"Okay," she barked, her voice suddenly hard, "turn and face the cabinet, and keep your hands where I can see them."

He slowly faced the glass case. She put one hand on Vic's shoulder and then self-assuredly commanded him, "Slowly open the case and hand me the gold necklace and earrings."

He carefully opened the case and gave her the jewelry.

"Now face the wall. I'll let you know when you are allowed to move," she ordered in a slightly less demanding voice, but no less convincing. A few minutes passed with quiet activity by Nadia, until she delivered her next order. She reached for his hands and whispered in his ear, "Now turn around." He spun to face her and gasped.

Nadia stood stark naked, except for the glittering necklace and earrings! She smiled and held his hands as she moved closer to him.

"Are you okay?" she asked seductively.

"Well," he whispered, "my heart is pounding like a drug dealer approaching a customs officer at the border..."

Nadia giggled and touched his chest.

"You know," he murmured, "You had me scared for a second. I thought you really had a gun in your purse."

"That's what I wanted you to think," she whispered mischievously, reaching up to kiss him.

Sounds of heavy breathing and sensual movements replaced any further conversation.

Quite a while later, they lay in bed together. Vic opened a drawer and took out a cigarette case and a metallic lighter. "Would you like one?" he asked. She smiled but shook her head. As he lit his cigarette, she noticed the lighter.

"Is that made of gold?" she asked.

Vic laughed. "It sure is! Another one of my finds. I had to clean it up and fill it with fluid, but it works perfectly!"

Nadia watched as he exhaled smoke in a sensual plume and reached up to trace his jaw with her finger. "A golden cigarette lighter. A golden life. You are too much."

He laughed. He smoked in lazy silence for a while, then took one final drag of his cigarette, dropping the filter with a hiss into the dregs of his wine. "How do you like your eggs cooked in the morning?" Vic asked. She sleepily murmured, "Whatever goes with these rocks." She drifted to sleep running her fingers over the necklace.

Beginning that night, Nadia and Vic were a couple. At first, their dates were only on weekends, but soon they became inseparable. Eating in chic restaurants and attending concerts and plays became routine for the pair. Before long, they ventured to Jamaica for pleasure and treasure hunting. Yet Nadia remained obsessed with the breathtaking necklace and earrings in Vic's case.

*Either marry Vic or steal them.* That's what Peter had said. Option one or option two?

In her mind, to marry a die-hard Buckeyes fan and live in Columbus was a lifetime torture. She simply couldn't imagine herself surrounded by people whom she literally hated from September to January. But for option two, she would require a partner. She needed help breaking into that solid cabinet. Finally, she made a decision.

One Saturday morning, Nadia took Vic to the airport for a flight to Denver, where his mother lived. He had given her the home security code so she could feed his dog. In the afternoon, she went to his house, opened the case and replaced the beloved jewelry with a fake set. It had taken her weeks to find someone willing to make cheap replicas from a photograph and then keep their mouths shut afterward. As she was leaving, she left a note for Vic, "I had a wonderful time with you. But I can't stay in this Buckeye town any longer. Hope you understand. You will be missed."

On Monday morning, Nadia entered the local cozy little Coffee Connection Cafe. The aroma of fresh coffee helped her to recover from last night's lack of sleep. As soon as Nadia sat down, an older gentleman approached her table with two cups of coffee.

"Good morning, Nadia."

"Good morning, Peter."

He took a sip of coffee. "Job well done."

Nadia answered with a wide grin, "Of course." Then she opened her purse and let Peter peek at its contents. He released a slight gasp when he saw the gleaming eighteen-karat necklace and matching earrings.

"Good. I'm here to collect the four thousand in cash you agreed to pay for my help."

Nadia handed him a large, nondescript envelope. "Here you go."

He quickly took it and rose from his seat. "Since this is a small town, I can't be seen with a pretty young woman for very long or tongues will wag."

Before leaving, Peter gave her a knowing wink. "By the way, you need to get rid of that hot merchandise promptly."

A few hours later, she visited Otie's, a bar-restaurant on a lively stretch of Main Street in the Columbus upper-class suburb of Hilliard. The area usually swells with boisterous bar crawlers on weekend nights, but this was a quiet weekday afternoon. Nadia took a seat at the bar. Now that her two-month-long caper was successfully completed, she wanted to relax. She asked the bartender to concoct his best-mixed drink.

He beamed. "How about a Golden Rose?"

"That sounds lovely. What's in it?

"Rose Petal Liqueur, Creme de Peche, Hibiscus and Cranberry Cordial, Cranberry Juice and a sprinkle of gold luster dust," he responded.

How appropriate, she thought to herself. She gave him a nod, "Sounds good."

While waiting for her drink, she glanced at the customers scattered around the bar. An old man with a salt and pepper beard and a cluster of empty bottles in front of him struggled to keep his eyes open. He had a Buddha's smile on his face. A woman in a pinstripe pantsuit shared a table with an older woman, pointing to items on the screen of a laptop and talking intently. At one end was a young couple watching an iPhone video and sharing a large plate of nachos.

"Here's your Golden Rose." The bartender proudly set the drink on the bar.

Sipping the unusual drink, Nadia began to unwind. But her mind, as always, was churning up the next step in her plan. Shortly, she noticed that a distinguished-looking older gentleman had seated himself two barstools away. He ordered a Johnny Walker Black on the rocks, and then started amiably talking to the bartender. After a few drinks, the gentleman related details of his life to the bored bartender. Being only a seat away Nadia happened to hear something very interesting. He was from India and was presently visiting his doctor son in Hilliard. In India, he was a goldsmith and owned a large jewelry store which specialized in selling and buying gold as well as diamond jewelry. Hearing the words gold, diamonds and jewelry, Nadia immediately turned and eyeballed him.

*This is the perfect man to wrap up my sting. There would be no trail. He is foreign, only here for a visit and appears quite respectable. What luck!*

Nadia moved next to him and introduced herself. "Hi. I'm Nadia. I overheard that you're from India. I've always wanted to visit such a fascinating country." She coyly smiled.

Delighted by the attention, he introduced himself. "I'm Narendra Soni. In my country "Soni" means "goldsmith". I make mountings for jewelry, especially diamonds, which my store sells and buys."

With her interest piqued, Nadia made her next inquiry. "I understand that India cuts and exports most of the world's diamonds. Is that true?"

Pompously, Narendra answered, "Yes, indeed! I can fulfill anyone's wish list. Would you like one, two, or three carats?" Then he smiled like a typical salesman.

Nadia asked the bartender for a refill and another scotch for Mr. Soni. When the bartender stepped away, she whispered, "Well, right now I'd like to sell a glamorous necklace. I actually have it locked in my car."

He frowned. "Why? Is it a stolen item?"

"Oh no, not at all," Nadia said smoothly. "My boyfriend gave it to me last Christmas, but we stopped seeing each other a month ago. I just don't want to keep anything which brings back past memories."

"Sorry to be rude. I have to be very careful. I could be charged with receiving stolen property. But I think you are a good girl. Come, I need to assess the necklace first. I have a test kit in my car."

They walked to a nearby parking lot and Mr. Soni fetched the kit from his vehicle. The necklace looked very authentic to him. He conducted an acid test in the back seat of Nadia's car.

"Oh, no. Oh dear. It looks like your ex-boyfriend was a conman. I'm sorry, but this is fake. We call it *fool's gold* and the diamonds are what we call *paste*. It is a good fake, but a fake nonetheless." He smiled faintly, thanked her for the drink, and exited the vehicle.

Nadia sat dumbfounded in the driver's seat. Frustration welled up in her and she pounded on the steering wheel. "Bastard!" she screamed. Months of planning for nothing! And she had paid that liar Peter four thousand dollars to help her!

The next evening, the familiar *vroom* of Vic's coupe cut through the twilight, as he arrived at the upscale French restaurant called The Refectory. Inside, Peter was waiting for him with a chilled bottle of Dom Perignon. He had a sly smile on his face.

"Cheers!" Peter welcomed him with a freshly-poured glass.

"Here, my friend. You deserve this. A thousand dollars for your services." Vic handed Peter an envelope. "That security app you put on my iPhone works like a charm. I activate it every night and also in my absence, causing my display case to revolve, hiding all of my genuine treasures and exposing the case full of fake replicas. Suggesting to Nadia that she should steal my necklace was brilliant. I was able to test the trustworthiness of my girlfriend and my security system at the same time! My valuables remained safe while I was out of town and I thank you. To tell you the truth, I never trusted her."

Peter laughed and put the money in his jacket as he heartily exclaimed, "Sometimes we all can be a Gold Digger, my friend!"

# Indian American Wedding

A few months ago, I received a phone call from my friend, Dilipbhai. In a downhearted voice, he said, "My daughter, Janki, just got engaged, and I want you to help us with the wedding plans. Can you come over to my house?" Traditional Indian weddings require much advance planning– just like an American wedding–but Indian weddings are also a community event.

Since I didn't hear any enthusiasm in his announcement, I immediately replied, "This is such good news. So why don't you sound excited? Is something wrong?"

"Oh, dear friend," he sighed. "My last child to marry has also turned away from her Indian heritage. She's engaged to another American." Dilipbhai had three lovely daughters. One daughter married a Caucasian and the oldest wed an African-American man. Dilipbhai believed in the traditional Hindu caste system and was hoping that even if she didn't marry in the same cast, at least her chosen mate would be an Indian man.

I resisted a laugh, and gently chided him, "Look, this is 2019. You need to expand your horizons. The world has gone global. I'll bet the shirt you are wearing was made in the Philippines, and that your pants were fabricated in China. Actually, you were even created in India and living in the USA!"

He quickly retorted, "My father was a farmer in India and he had two sons-in-law. They would help him for entire days under the hot sun without balking. They would never try to change his routine." He paused for a minute and added, "Now my sons-in-law come here and immediately change my Bollywood channel to a football game. Then they give me orders, 'Hey Dad, can you toss me a beer?' Sometimes I get so angry that I want to spill the entire contents over their heads."

His wife, Mina, overheard our conversation and quickly interjected, "Well, well! You love them dearly when one shovels our driveway in the cold winter and the other mows the lawn in the hot summer."

About five months before the wedding, a few family members and friends met to go over the wedding details.

"Okay, so. How will the groom get to the wedding?" asked an uncle.

"We need to book a limousine right now," spoke up one of the groom's college buddies. "Graduations will be at the same time of the month."

Of course, he was correct, but Dilipbhai's head snapped up and he said sharply, "Listen to me very carefully. There is no way that my future son-in-law will arrive to his wedding in a limousine! My grandfather rode an elephant when he got married.

My father and I both rode horses." He smacked his hand on the coffee table for emphasis. "Even my two American sons-in-law, dressed in traditional Indian garments, managed to straddle their horses. This incoming son-in-law must ride a horse to the wedding."

Considering New Jersey traffic, I beseeched him to change his mind. But Dilipbhai steadfastly refused to eliminate his family tradition. One young man promptly searched the internet for horse rentals. I advised him, "Son, please make sure it's not a circus horse; they will walk in circles only." After some searching and a few phone calls, he found a place and booked a horse and handler for two hours.

The second quest before the gathering of amateur wedding planners was to find a priest who could speak three languages fluently. Traditionally, a cleric only needed to speak Sanskrit and a regional Indian language. However, since this was to be a combination of Eastern and Western cultures, all the Hindu rituals and philosophy needed to be explained to the groom and other guests in English. Everyone agreed to invite a Brahmin Professor named Trivedi to perform the ceremony.

Next, we moved on to the selection of a photographer. From my personal experience, I suggested they hire a professional photographer. Once I asked a friend to take pictures of my daughter's sixteenth birthday party. This friend had shown up with his own family in tow. As a result, the album of my daughter's special day was full of the photographer's family's candid pictures, and none of my daughter's smiling face!

Finally, everything was planned and scheduled. A large hall was reserved for the wedding, where a beautiful stage would be decorated with roses, chrysanthemums and gerberas. Floral chandeliers would dazzle above the venue's tables. The three hundred invited guests could expect a sumptuous menu.

Once the preparations were complete, time seemed to pass quickly. On the day of the wedding, more than fifty women and girls in their colorful saris gathered outside of the hall to greet the groom on his mount. Bollywood wedding songs played from a loudspeaker. People danced to the music until someone shouted, "The groom's party is approaching!"

I looked down the street and noticed that an old man from our group had become the self-appointed traffic cop. The hired horse handler was guiding the groom's steed toward the wedding hall. The groom wore a traditional turban decorated with flowers. Both he and the horse were dressed in shimmering red and gold finery. The groom's *baraat* included his family and friends, especially Indian college pals. This part of the wedding was about fun and not religion. The American groom was doing his best to embrace these unfamiliar traditions, and tried to sit, upright and proud, on his wedding steed.

Everyone was happy, singing, and dancing to loud music. People in colorful clothes filled the street. The procession moved slowly toward the hall. The horse abruptly stopped upon entering the parking lot. He seemed confused by all the bright colors and loud music. He wouldn't move, even after a gentle nudge from his trainer's crop. All the colorful bling and the booming melodies were totally unfamiliar to him. The horse whinnied and shied, and then, suddenly, a flood of liquid! The horse was urinating. The women screamed and recoiled as the pee splashed on their brightly colored silk saris. People began to shout and back away from the beast. One older woman—the bride's aunt—vehemently cursed the horse and handler in her native language. The festive scene had become mayhem.

Unaware of what was happening outside the hall, Professor Trivedi, the officiating priest, was getting anxious. He was scheduled for another wedding ceremony immediately after this function. Impatiently, he declared, "If the groom doesn't get inside in five minutes, the holy hour will be missed, and the marriage will have the curse of divorce in six months!" Immediately, someone ran out to fetch the groom.

In the parking lot, the horse remained immobilized by fear. After receiving the priest's warning, the elderly man, in charge of delivering the groom inside, shouted to the handler, "Either the groom gets in the hall within five minutes, or you won't receive any payment." The trainer sharply swatted the poor horse's rear with the crop to get it moving, but the horse reared up like a stallion in an old Western movie—and began to defecate! Horse feces flying through the air was too much. The crowd panicked, fleeing the parking lot, and erupted, shrieking, into the event hall. The shocked groom, watching his wedding fall apart, tried to escape the offensive horse by sliding off, and crashed to the pavement, twisting an ankle. A few friends helped him to get inside. They sat him down to assess the injury.

"It's not swelling. Can you move it?" asked one of his friends who was crouched near his feet.

"Yeah," grunted the groom, wincing. "I think I'm okay. I can walk."

"Hey," called another college buddy, trying to get the attention of someone across the event hall, "tell the priest we are good to go."

It seemed that there was no permanent damage. As I sat in the audience and waited, I studied Dilipbhai as he watched the groom gingerly make his way to his proper spot in the ceremony. Dilipbhai looked around, took it all in–the chaos, the humor, the love. Something changed in his face at that moment.

The rest of the wedding proceeded without any unforeseen complications. Janki was radiant. The reception was full of dancing, music and a grand feast. Dilipbhai sat in the middle of a circle of his sons-in-law, drinking whiskey and chatting about upcoming Redskins versus Eagles football game.

Finally, around midnight, the party ended and I headed out to my car. As I entered the lot, I noticed that the elderly man who had been in charge of traffic control was arguing with a young man who seemed to speak mostly Spanish.

"Look, man," said the young man, "twenty-five dollars is not enough to clean up this mess. This poop is from a horse, not a dog! I'm going to need a shovel!"

Enraged, the older man replied, "Yesterday you agreed in writing to clean the parking lot of rubbish for twenty-five dollars. It doesn't matter what animal decided to poop here."

But the young man would not change his position about the work. I know some Spanish so I decided to try and intervene. Approaching the young man, I said, "*Amigo, gracias a dios, no trajimos elephant.*"

The young worker's eyebrows shot up, and a look of realization crossed his face. He responded quickly. "Oh, no! No, senior." and he immediately started to clean the lot. I winked at the elderly man and walked to my car. Surprised, he ran after me and asked, "What did you tell him? I've been trying for an hour to convince him to clean up that mess. But he just wouldn't listen."

I started my car, rolled down the window, and relayed what I had told the young man.

"Hey buddy, just thank God we didn't bring an elephant."

# LUCK OF THE IRISH

He stood on a platform at Union Station. Even though he was currently unemployed and had no real prospects, he wore a black wool overcoat, dress slacks, and wingtips. He carried a briefcase. These elements were essentially a costume, borrowed from a friend. It was time for his luck to change.

He was born on the thirty-first of December. Every year, people would tell him how lucky he was to have a birthday on New Year's Eve. The whole world would celebrate on that day, but he never liked his birth date. Growing up, his birthday parties were always overshadowed by New Year's Eve gatherings. People would pay less attention to him and more to the champagne and the glittering ball dropping in Times Square on their television screens.

He always thought that good luck was not part of his life. He failed to gain admission to law school and ended up a drama major at a liberal arts school. He graduated, but his acting career never really got off the ground. He usually landed minor roles with small shows, and they always seemed to have short runs. Once, when he was in his early twenties, though, his luck seemed to change. He got the main part for a major Broadway drama. He leapt at the opportunity and worked hard to perfect his character and performance. Then, two days before opening night, he woke up with a swollen throat and a fever. The doctor diagnosed a virus, and the part went to his understudy. Yet, he never gave up, and always thought that one day he would hit the jackpot and achieve on-stage fame and success. That life dream was with him constantly. The only other person in his life that held on to this hope was his late grandmother. After she passed away, he missed having someone to believe in him. He promised himself that he would dedicate his first major role to her.

Grandma had once given him a full-length mirror. It was a simple and beautiful with a delicate filigree design of gold and silver. He enjoyed gazing at himself each morning as he prepared for his daily job search. He was tall and lean with good muscle tone. His physique gave the impression of confidence, which seemed lately to belie the truth. He had sensuous lips, glittering blue eyes, an aquiline nose, and a full head of sandy hair. He was definitely a good-looking man.

Not only did his physical appearance lead him to believe that he would eventually succeed, his voice was deep and imposing—a performer's voice. It was a mix of John Wayne, Clint Eastwood, and Al Pacino. People noticed the resemblance, and he loved it. They were all his idols. He had watched their movies countless times. When home alone, he would occasionally put on in his cowboy hat and do a John Wayne impersonation in his mirror, or clench his teeth and utter Clint Eastwood's famous line, "Go ahead, make my day". When he did Brando from "The Godfather," people in the next room swore it sounded like someone had turned on the movie.

He finally decided to prove his ability to take on a character's persona by completely becoming that character. This was why he was standing in Washington's Union Station on a wintry Monday afternoon. He had devised a plan to convince a stranger that he was someone else. Having decided that his new name would be Mr. Richard Lyons, a successful Washington attorney, he waited anxiously to board the train to New York.

After taking his seat on the train, he realized that his seat mate was a young woman avidly poring over a style magazine, who didn't seem to present much of a challenge. He tried to engage her in conversation but was met with a blank stare. All her energy was focused on the magazine in her lap. He changed seats next to an older, scholarly looking woman. Unfortunately, she began to chatter about herself, with no hesitation in sight. There would be no opportunity to practice his deceit with her. He wasn't even able to provide the woman with more than a cursory introduction.

So when the train left the station, he made his way to the lounge car. The room was full of men and women in business suits, sipping lattes or cocktails as they read newspapers and made phone calls. Finally, "Mr. Lyons" spotted the perfect candidate. He was a well-dressed, middle-aged man reading the Wall Street Journal. Quickly, he took the empty club chair next to this gentleman. The gentleman glanced up and smiled, then went back to reading.

"Nice day," said the fake Mr. Lyons, opening his briefcase and flipping through a folder of papers.

"It is," smiled the man, looking up for a moment and sipping his coffee. The actor put out his hand.

"I'm Richard. Have to stop over in New York for a case."

"Herbert. You seem pretty busy. You an attorney?"

The ostensible Mr. Lyons nodded. "Defense. And boy, I can't believe it's only Monday; I'm totally exhausted. I was in court every day last week representing some very high profile clients both as defendants and plaintiffs. Preparations for these cases, including briefs, can also involve hours of my time. A few weeks ago I pled a case before the Virginia State Supreme Court. It was quite a challenging case, but I nailed it during my cross-examination of a witness."

Herbert nodded with interest. "Sounds like your client was lucky to have you in that courtroom."

Herbert believed everything that Attorney Lyons related to him. The conversation continued, and the older gentleman ordered drinks and a tray of tapas for them. For two hours, Mr. Lyons regaled him with tales of the exciting cases he had handled over the years. He enthusiastically claimed to have won both criminal and civil cases. This pseudo-attorney naturally blamed Washington's politics on the snail-like progression of justice.

Eventually, he gave a big sigh and quoted a famous line in a dramatic way, "In my book, justice delayed is justice denied."

The other gentleman was so impressed that he shouted, "Bravo!" and ordered him another drink.

*I am truly an actor,* the young man thought to himself.

"Ladies and Gentleman, we will be arriving in New York in ten minutes."

Hearing the announcement, both men started walking towards the exit. Just as they were about to disembark, the sham lawyer turned to the other gentleman, "I am so sorry, I was chattering away about my work never asked you about yourself. What do you do?"

"I'm a movie producer here in New York," he answered. "I am always looking for a good talent. If you weren't such a successful attorney, with your youth, looks, and voice, you'd probably have great success on becoming a movie star in one of my projects."

The actor's jaw dropped, but before he could respond, the older gentleman disappeared into the train station's bustling crowd.

# RECYCLE

It was an unusually hot September afternoon in Philadelphia. After finishing some routine Saturday morning errands, Amit pulled his car into the driveway. He turned off the car's engine, and then noticed that his wife and granddaughter were in front of the house, sorting through piles of things. The lawn was strewn with clothing, kitchenware and small appliances, old books, and outgrown toys. Amit loved that his daughter and her family lived so close. He saw his granddaughter, Meena, at least every other weekend. Earlier that month, he had taken her to the history museum in the city. They had walked along the echoing halls, fascinated by displays of pottery, armor from ancient battles, important books and documents, and relics from monumental events in history. She was always full of questions and ideas. Just like today–here she was, digging through their dusty old belongings.

"Hey precious, what are you doing?" he called out.

Enthusiastically, Meena replied, "We learned about recycling in my class at school last week, and I'm helping Grandma separate everything in the garage and attic that can be reprocessed."

"Good job," he said, smiling. Then he went inside the house and put away the groceries. When he came outside again, he noticed that Meena was climbing down the ladder from the storage area above the garage. She gingerly maintained her balance while clutching a bulky suitcase. "Please be careful," Amit cautioned.

"Don't worry, Grandpa," she said confidently. "I know what I'm doing." A moment later, he heard, "Look at what I found, Grandma."

"Leave that one alone. It's your grandfather's favorite," her grandmother snickered.

"What's in it?" Meena queried, as she attempted to open the bag.

The bag was gaudy: brown leather with black stripes. Amit sat down next to the child and said, "This is the suitcase I brought with me the first time I arrived from India forty years ago!" Right away, they decided to look inside. The lock had jammed over the many years, but after prying it with a screwdriver, the case opened. The faint scent of exotic curry powder drifted out.

"Eww!" His granddaughter backed away from the case with a disgusted look on her face. Even though the odor was unsavory to her, it was nostalgic to Amit. The aroma swiftly seeped into his brain, and as he examined the old newspapers in the case, he slipped backward in time.

All the wrinkles and grey hair vanished. He was transformed into a twenty–two-year-old man, shopping with his sister in India on a hot summer day. Only one day remained before his departure to the United States.

"*Sahib*, you need this bag," the pushy shop keeper declared. "It is big and sturdy, but very lightweight. Everyone going to America buys this one. You must get this for your journey."

"Don't give us such drivel," his sister snapped. "That suitcase is sufficient, but not worth the price that you're asking for it. Look at the colors! We won't pay the full price for something so gaudy." She began to haggle, eventually departing triumphant with a twenty-five percent discount.

Jokingly, Amit commented, "Sis, one day when I become the CEO of a company, I will appoint you as the Finance Manager."

"We'll discuss that when the time arrives," she replied, "but for now, just treat me to a tasty lunch."

That night, all the relatives gathered in the living room around the recently purchased suitcase. Everything that he was planning to take with him to America was spread throughout the room. Clothes, personal articles, gifts, and books must all fit in that single suitcase. Although it was very, very large, he wasn't sure everything would fit. Then, one by one, all the neighbors and family friends came by to wish him goodbye. Other than gifts for him, they also brought things for their sons and daughters in the United States. Somehow, he must take all these items with him.

Amid all of the hubbub, Grandma emerged from the kitchen and handed him a small package.

"What is in it?" someone demanded loudly.

Grandma smiled. "His favorite curry powder. I made it today with fresh ingredients, especially for Amit." Everyone started talking at once.

"No, he can't take that!"

"The smell will ruin his new clothes. Take it back."

Although she pleaded, no one listened to her. Everyone spent the next few hours packing, unpacking, arranging and rearranging everything until it fit. Finally, after midnight, the bag was packed, and they all went to bed.

At least one hundred people took the train to see him off at Bombay Airport. He turned to the crowd of loved ones one final time, smiling and waving. Then, his eyes blurred with tears, he boarded the plane and left India.

Much later, Amit stood in the New York airport, nearly delirious from his twenty-four-hour-long flight. Suddenly he heard hooting and shouting.

"Amit!"

He whirled around to see his two friends. They ran up to him, hugging him and shaking his shoulders.

Although he was exhausted and dragging around an enormous, heavy suitcase, they wanted to introduce him to some real American food right away. They walked up the street to the Pizza Palace where they each purchased a slice of pizza. His friends raved about the doughy triangle covered with red sauce, cheese and bits of pepper, onion, mushrooms and olives. In truth, Amit found it unappetizing compared to Grandma's spicy Indian cooking, but he resisted telling that to his companions. After a bus and subway ride, they took turns dragging the heavy suitcase up three stories to his friends' apartment. That night, upon opening the suitcase, he noticed a small package, carefully wrapped in newspaper and tucked way down in a corner. When he unwrapped and opened it, the small room was filled with the aroma of curry powder. He smiled. "Grandma..." That night Amit was sleepless, as tearful thoughts unfolded of all the family and friends which he had left behind. His grandma's thoughtful offering gently reminded him of those loving, familiar faces that were now so far away.

"Grandpa...Grandpa!" Someone was shouting at him. All of a sudden, he became a sixty-two-year-old man again. He wiped away the tears and went inside to wash his face. By the time he had composed himself and returned to the garage, the suitcase was no longer there.

"Where is the case?" he shouted frantically.

His granddaughter answered proudly, "I recycled it! I gave it to the recycle truck man."

"What? Where did he go?" he roared, rushing out to the sidewalk to look around. Just then, he saw a big truck starting to leave the area and head in the direction of the interstate. Even though he was barefoot, Amit started running after it. He shouted as loudly as possible, "Stop!! Please stop!!" Finally, the truck had to wait for a traffic light.

"Excuse me?" Amit waved his arms until the driver glanced over.

"What?" the driver yelled over the noise of traffic, getting ready to shift gears and drive away.

"Please pull over! I need something that got put in your truck!"

The driver looked doubtful, so Amit, almost in tears, pulled out his wallet and waved a ten-dollar bill. Moments later, the truck was on the shoulder, back open, with Amit and the driver digging through the pile of junk. Amit shoved a bundle of cardboard to one side and there it was! The suitcase!

"Thank you so much, sir!" Amit said, pressing the money into the driver's hand.

"Yeah, you're welcome." The driver seemed uncertain how to react to this odd man. "Uh, hope you have a good day." With a winner's smile, Amit walked back home, tightly holding the suitcase.

As soon as he entered the house, his wife's harsh words greeted him, "Do you realize that you made a fool of yourself in the neighborhood? Everyone was watching as you ran after a garbage truck to retrieve a shabby old suitcase."

Amit simply ignored her and sat down on the sofa. Meena brought a glass of water. "Thank you, sweetie." He took a few sips. "Now darling, recycling is a great concept. However, in life, not everything is made to be recycled. There are certain things which need to be preserved forever."

Pausing, he looked into the young girl's eyes, and asserted, "That's why museums exist."

# A Ski Trip

Andy's heart sank as he watched Joe, who had been staggering through the snow in front of him, suddenly drop to his knees. Andy rushed to him. "Joe! Are you okay?"

Joe's breathing was ragged and his head lolled with exhaustion. "I...I can't do this. Just leave me here." He collapsed to all fours, then fell face down in the snow. He moaned softly.

Andy got down next to him and took his hand. "Come on, Joe. Don't just give up like that. Remember that fishing trip when the motor failed a good mile out in the ocean? It was so hot, and there was no radio, and we were almost out of drinking water. You said, 'Andy, we've got to swim this.' I was struggling in the water, man, struggling bad. I thought I was gonna die out there. But you wouldn't let me quit. Kept talking about Marsha and Todd and Laney. You gave me that shot of adrenaline I needed, and somehow I got to shore. So now you're gonna climb this hill for me."

Andy and Joe were high school chums. As they approached their mid-forties, Andy was a married father of two and Joe still enjoyed the single life. Every other year, they would take a trip together: climbing mountains, deep sea fishing, or, as on this trip, skiing. It was late January, a beautiful time in the Rockies. After two days on the slopes of this resort, they decided they wanted to try out 13,041-foot Grand Traverse Peak, which was about seven miles east of Vail, Colorado and known for great backwoods skiing. But after making several wrong turns, and without a functioning GPS or cell service, they were hopelessly lost. They drove the winding roads until they ran out of gas and then bundled up and abandoned the car. Now, in the winter dusk, they were on a long, cold trek back to civilization.

After a week's worth of snowfall and steadily dropping temperatures, conditions were brutal. Moonlight projecting on the white snow provided them with some direction. However, when a cloud hid the moon, the night would become nearly pitch black.

Finally, they reached a hilltop. Now they were able to see a small town at the base. The houses dotted the patchwork of several good-sized farms. They squinted into the distance, looking for signs of activity. Andy spotted a light in one of the farmhouses. "Look, Joe, someone's awake. Just keep thinking about having hot food and coffee." Descending the hill was easy and only took twenty minutes to reach the lit house at the base of the mountain. They kept praying that the homeowner wouldn't switch them off and go to bed.

The men stiffly stomped up onto the porch with frozen legs. They glanced at one another briefly, then Andy pushed the doorbell. *Please please please*, thought Joe. There was movement inside the house. Andy shivered and pushed the bell again. Foosteps approached the door, and it opened a few inches. A tall, beautiful woman peered at them past the chain lock.

"I am so sorry to bother you, ma'am," said Andy, "but we are lost and need shelter." She gazed at them for a moment, then closed the door. Both men's shoulders slumped until they heard her releasing the chain lock on the door. It swung open again, revealing the woman in a flowing, white nightgown, with a glass of red wine in her hand. She looked to be in her late thirties, and had sadness in her eyes. "I live by myself," she replied warily. "I don't feel comfortable letting people that I don't know stay inside the house, but you're welcome to spend the night in the barn out back. I'll make some sandwiches and coffee for you."

Andy and Joe trekked around to the well-kept barn behind the house. Andy released the latch and put his hip against the door. It was pitch dark inside until he turned on the flashlight on his phone. Inside was a tractor, a riding lawn mower, stacks of straw bales, a few wooden pallets. Joe found a switch on the wall that turned on two bare bulbs that were dangling over their heads. It was much warmer inside the barn, but by no means cozy.

"Hey, I think we're gonna live!" Joe laughed.

"Could be a lot worse," agreed Andy. At that moment, the door creaked open, and the woman appeared with two sleeping bags and two blankets.

"Thank you so much, ma'am," said Andy, smiling at her. "I know this sounds dramatic, but we were really worried we were going to freeze to death out there."

The woman half-smiled and nodded. "Glad you didn't," she said shortly. "The coffee is brewing. I'll bring you some sandwiches in a few minutes." She was true to her word, and soon they were sipping steaming coffee and munching on sandwiches made with thick homemade bread, cold sliced chicken, mustard, and tomatoes. The food made the men drowsy, so they unrolled the sleeping bags and settled in for the night. The next morning, Andy and Joe woke early and departed quietly, not wanting to awaken the kind woman who had helped them. They started off to find someone who could help retrieve the SUV.

After a frigid January, winter turned into a beautiful spring, followed by a blazing summer. During barbecues with friends, they would laughingly relate their ski trip adventure and night in the barn.

Fall eventually burst out in a colorful display. One October afternoon, about nine months after their trip, Joe received a thick envelope in the mail. He looked at the sender's address and noticed that it came from an attorney in Colorado. As he read the contents, his eyes widened.

"What the heck?" he yelled. He sat down, thinking through the night they had been stranded, recalling the mysterious beauty and the shelter she had offered. He read the letter again more slowly and even though he was alone, yelled out, "Andy!" He rushed out of the door and, without even calling, drove to his house.

Joe pounded on the door until Andy opened it, looking alarmed.

"What the heck, man?" demanded Andy.

Joe waved the envelope in his face. "We need to talk."

Andy ushered him into the living room. "No one's home, Marsha and the kids are at soccer. What's up with the envelope?"

"What happened that I don't know about the night we stayed in that woman's barn?"

Andy froze. The color drained from his face. "Nothing happened. What are you talking about?"

Joe glared at him. "Andy!" He held up the envelope. Andy's shoulders sagged.

"I can't lie to you," sighed Andy. "You're my best friend. That night I felt cold in the barn so I went back to the house for more blankets. Sarah invited me in for a glass of wine and we chatted. She had lost her husband in a car accident a few months before and was feeling very sad and lonely. Unfortunately, she had no other relatives or close friends. Her sadness really touched me, so I comforted her, and we ended up finishing the bottle together." By this time they had moved to the kitchen table and Andy stopped to sip some coffee.

Joe sighed impatiently. "Come on! What happened next?"

Andy avoided Joe's eyes. "I'm sorry Joe. I screwed up. I wanted to stay in touch with her, but I didn't want Marsha to find out, so I gave her your name and address as mine. Then I never heard from her and so I just put the whole thing out of my mind."

After a long pause, Joe uttered, "Hmm...that answers the question as to why this letter was sent to me."

With shame and guilt on his face, Andy whispered, "I'm so sorry. You're my closest friend. I'll take full responsibility for what I did that night. I'll pay for whatever she needs."

Holding the envelope tightly, Joe walked out of the house. Andy followed him and implored, "Please Joe, at least tell me if it's a boy or a girl."

Smiling, Joe looked at him. "Relax. There is no boy or girl. As it turns out, Sarah passed away last month and left all her assets, including that lovely house and big farm to the man named Joe."

Then he winked at him and said, "But since you're not Joe, I guess that I get everything. Thanks, good friend."

# UNCOUTH

Rita arrived at the airport with plenty of time to check her baggage and go through security. One of her strongest attributes was promptness, and she never accepted tardiness in herself or others. In fact, she didn't tolerate anything or anybody which she considered "uncouth". Rita had her own set of life rules, and above all, she was fastidious. This was manifested in how she dressed. Her suit was by Chanel, shoes by Jimmy Choo, and the magenta purse she carried was a Gucci original, all from the current season's collection, of course. Her hair was dark, short, stylish, and perfectly coiffed. The toenails peeking out of fashionable sling-back shoes were polished to an impeccable, shiny red. There was no wrinkle, spot, or tear. Everything about Rita oozed "couth."

She found a seat in the waiting area for her gate and began to observe the other passengers. People-watching made her edgy because other people's flaws made her feel uncomfortable, but she couldn't stop herself. This could be in their clothes, language or manners. She immediately noticed a heavy-set, middle-aged woman dressed in a very revealing jumpsuit. Although the woman had an attractive face, Rita felt her outfit was definitely not appropriate. She spotted another example of her rules being broken by the young girl sitting across from her. She was typing happily on her iPad with multicolored fingernails. Rita cringed at the sight. To further unnerve her, the man at the end of the row wore a pair of flimsy sandals over mismatched socks. She saw some people running to the gates, dragging their suitcases to catch a flight. She shook her head and uttered to herself, "Idiots. Why don't they plan better and come early to the airport? Like I do."

In order to distract herself from her self-torturous game, Rita began a conversation with the lady seated next to her. "This looks like a crowded flight. Do you fly often?" Just as the woman smiled and started to speak, Rita let out a little gasp. The woman's teeth had multiple pieces of dark green food lodged between them! Luckily, the loudspeaker interrupted any further conversation with an announcement. The upcoming flight would be delayed.

After she discovered that the interval before boarding the plane would take longer than she had anticipated, her one deviance from perfection began to surface in her mind. A few strides away from her gate were the legendary Golden Arches with their greasy, salty, delicious French fries waiting inside. The smell was alluring. Her stomach rumbled. In moments she had caved to temptation and gotten in line at the restaurant. The service was quick and efficient (she certainly noticed and approved) and she glided to the seating area to find herself a table. The empty one she chose had some residual grease, so she snapped open her ever-present packet of wipes and began to clean the table with brisk movements. A family of five arrived and occupied the next table. Rita shuddered at the likelihood that she would have to witness the small children's untidy eating habits.

"Excuse me, ma'am." Rita glanced up from her table-scrubbing to see a woman standing nearby. "May I take the extra chair from your table? We're a little short over there."

"Yes, of course," replied Rita, secretly happy that she had relieved her of any possibility that she would end up sitting across from some stranger. Just as she took the first French fry from the box, her cell phone rang. It was her son calling from San Francisco, and the connection was very bad. She hurriedly shifted her bag to her shoulder and walked near the window for a better reception. While talking to her son, Sam, she turned and glanced back at her table and gasped.

"Hey! You! Get away from my food!" People turned to stare as she dashed back across the room to her table, which was now occupied by the most disheveled, dirty man that she had ever seen. He was sitting in her chair and eating her French fries! This was certainly the epitome of uncouth!

"How dare you?" she practically screamed, "Those are my fries! I bought them! You can't just take something that isn't yours."

The man seemed to be quite flustered by the outburst and failed to move. He looked puzzled and then turned the box toward her as though offering to share. He said something in a language she did not understand and smiled kindly. He pointed at himself, then at her. He took a fry, then extended the box to her as though offering a flower. Of course, Rita was completely taken aback by such an unkempt man's action. Now that he had his dirty fingers in the container, she didn't even want them back, let alone to share them with him!

Since she was still holding the phone, she could hear Sam speaking. "What's wrong?" he kept asking.

"I can't believe this," she responded with annoyance. "When I was talking with you, some man sat down at my table and has begun eating my fries."

"Really?" Sam could barely contain a laugh. "What does he look like?"

Her answer was filled with disgust. "Oh, some elderly man with a long white beard and rumpled clothing. And he doesn't speak English!"

"There are plenty of nice non-English-speaking people on this Earth, Mom. Several billion, I would guess."

Rita responded sharply, "That may be true, but he is eating my French fries!" Then she crossly added, "And I don't even know how to tell him to stop. People shouldn't be allowed into the country unless they can communicate."

In response, Sam admonished her, "Come on Mom, don't be so ridiculous. He is probably just visiting his family in the States. All visitors can't speak English. Did you speak Spanish when you traveled to Mexico last year?"

Begrudgingly, she replied, "OK. Mr. Know-it-all. My flight is called. I have to hang up now. Love you."

"Have a safe trip, Mom, and please relax," her son said, then added with a laugh, "Try not to dwell on the French fries incident."

As she boarded the plane, she still had the image in her head of the grime on the man's fingers as he picked up her fries and devoured them. It was definitely not done in her dainty style. "What an uncouth person," she uttered for about the fifth time.

Before Rita sat down, she opened her purse to put her ticket away and did a double take. "Oh no!" she shrieked as a flood of embarrassed realization coursed through her.

There beside her faithful packet of wipes was a box of cold French fries, right where she had stuffed them when her phone had started to ring.

# GODS OF THE UNIVERSE

Professor Arif stood in front of the mirror and straightened his tie. He was a distinguished, slender, fifty-year-old man with emerald-green eyes, salt-and-pepper hair, and a wisp of a goatee beard. Originally from Turkey, Arif had lived in the United States for the last twenty-five years.

"How do I look, Honey?" He always asked his wife, Selma, this before leaving the house, but today she would be leaving with him.

She smiled affectionately and adjusted his tie. "Professor, you always look terrific to me. Now let's go. We don't want to be late on your special day."

After ten years of research and labor, he proudly published a book titled *Gods of the Universe*. Today would be its debut launch at Chattanooga's Westin Hotel. He was held in high regard in the academic world, and there was a lot of publicity about the book, so not only his family, friends, and students would be there to honor his accomplishment, but also the public that admired his work.

Following stop-and-go traffic through downtown, they arrived at the hotel ten minutes behind schedule. The venue was quite crowded with people waiting to hear him and obtain a copy of his book. Arif was always admired for his broad knowledge, his concise explanations, and the little touch of humor he always sprinkled in. After shaking hands with some college dignitaries, he took the podium, adjusted his glasses, and began a brief speech.

"Thank you all for coming here to help me launch this book. I will make my remarks cursory. First of all, I want to thank my family," he paused and gestured toward where his wife was sitting, "my peers and fellow researchers for your patience and support, and my students for being sounding boards for my ideas over the years. This has been a long journey, but at last we have the finished product! Let's have a little taste of it, shall we? A little appetizer." The crowd chuckled and there were a few scattered claps. "As you already know, my book is a definitive work, as well as a new look at the deities of the different religions, cultures and mythologies of the world, including those gods personified as animals." He paused to have a sip of water and then continued.

"By one estimate, there are forty-two thousand religions in the world today. Of course, there is at least one, or even several, gods in each religion. I'm going to comment on a few today. There are seven major religions around the world. These are Animism, Hinduism, Buddhism, Judaism, Christianity, Islam and Sikhism. Buddhism doesn't have a god, so we'll eliminate it from today's comments.

"Greek myths always refer to a small group of twelve powerful gods called the Olympians. Mount Olympus is where they would meet. Besides these twelve, there were many other groupings of twelve gods throughout ancient Greece. The stories of the Olympian Twelve's battles, jealousies, insecurities and pettiness have influenced the course of the Western language and narrative.

"Early Christian views of God were expressed in the Pauline Epistles and the early creeds, which proclaimed one God and the divinity of Jesus. Christianity, of course, developed as a part of Judaism. Christianity regarded Jesus as God's presence in human form, whereas, this was unacceptable to Jews.

"Hinduism is a pantheistic religion. It equates God with the universe. Yet, this religion is also polytheistic because it is populated by a myriad of gods and goddesses who personify aspects of the one true God. This allows individuals to worship based on a family tradition, community and regional practices and other considerations. There are thirty-three million gods and goddesses in this religion, although there are three main ones. They are Brahma the Creator, Vishnu the preserver, Shiva the destroyer." The audience was listening, nodding.

"What many people don't realize is how much these ancient beliefs and practices have become woven into our modern existence. Not just in our spiritual practice and philosophy, but our day-to-day lives. The rhythms and patterns of these ancient religions are present in the most logical, secular elements of our civilization. Technology, science, politics, economics. It is like a hidden code, a hidden truth." He paused. He had the audience on the edge of their seats. "Well, I could continue for at least two more hours, but then you wouldn't buy my book! So I'll stop here and let the celebration begin."

He gestured toward the tables in the back of the room, which were spread with ornate platters of exotic desserts. "My lovely wife has arranged for sweets from all around the world to be available for our refreshment. Please help yourself." Then he jokingly added, "Although it is interesting to note that all of these religions have one thing in common. They all advise that we refrain from gluttony." Again, there was a wave of light laughter and the audience began to stand up and circulate.

People lined up for at Professor Arif's table with their newly-purchased books to have them autographed. The professor was chatting and signing books when he heard a high-pitched, squeaky voice behind him.

"Hello Arif, do you remember me?" He turned to see the owner of such an annoying voice and encountered a rotund woman in her late forties. He didn't recognize her at first, but that peculiar voice and aquiline nose threw him into the past.

The year became 1990. He had just arrived in the United States from Turkey on a student visa. He was continuing his studies in Chattanooga at the University of Tennessee. He was a twenty-five-year-old man who eagerly desired a date with an American girl.

One day after a philosophy class, he met a girl named Vivian. She was very sexy with blonde hair and lovely blue eyes. She had a small frame and was slim with a few curves. Her voice was somewhat squeaky and she had a rather prominent nose. All in all, she had a friendly personality and they hit it off right away. Although his friends warned him about her love of upscale, expensive restaurants,

Arif decided to ask her for a date. Arif was a naturally generous man, but since he was on a student visa, he had a very limited budget. So he devised a plan to keep down the cost of a date without losing his dignity.

The next week, he asked Vivian to accompany him to a Turkish restaurant. Arif knew the owner and had already enlisted his help. No expensive dishes would be available for them. On the way to the restaurant, he tried to influence her with details about tasty and healthy Turkish food. The restaurant was small, but tastefully decorated with authentic Turkish rugs and beautiful mosaic vases. Traditional Turkish music played in the background. Upon being seated, Vivian promptly asked for the wine list. Since this was a small, family restaurant, they didn't have a liquor license. Right away, Vivian's mood changed and she told him, "I'm sorry, but I always drink wine with my meals."

Since Arif didn't want to cause a scene, and was determined to please her on the first date, they moved on to her favorite ritzy French restaurant, La Cabriole. It was a former church with soaring ceilings and vibrant stained-glass windows. The ambience was cozy, with dimmed lighting and tables illuminated by small candles placed next to fresh flower vases. Prints of magnificent paintings by Van Gogh and Monet hung on the walls. On a small stage there was a young, long-haired man softly playing the guitar. The hostess took them to a private table in a corner. Vivian held his hand and whispered, "Isn't this such a romantic place?" He managed a smile, although he was terrified of how expensive the menu was likely to be.

A smiling waitress with long black hair welcomed them and offered a wine list. While

Vivian tried to decide on a wine to order, Arif quickly glanced at the menu. The prices of the *hors d'oeuvres* alone sent shock waves through him. *What? Roasted goat cheese for fifteen dollars? In a Turkish restaurant it costs five dollars and back home Mom gets fine goat cheese for less than two.* He excused himself and hurried to the restroom to wash his hands. He actually wanted to review the amount of cash in his wallet. It was enough for the Turkish restaurant, but definitely not adequate for a high-class place such as the one he now found himself inside. Luckily, he had also brought his checkbook.

By the time he returned to the table, Vivian had already ordered an expensive bottle of wine and an appetizer of sashimi tuna and salmon Gravad Lax with Herruga caviar. Even considering the financial circumstances, he decided to try and enjoy the evening with this desirable woman. He leaned towards her in the dimness, and peered into her clear, blue eyes. He had to admit that she did look very appealing and so he whispered, "You are quite lovely."

Completely ignoring the compliment, she abruptly asked him, "What's your major?"

Taken aback, he replied, "Philosophy. But let's not talk about school here," he said as the server brought the wine and appetizers.

As the evening progressed, Arif wanted to get both physically and intellectually closer, but Vivian was too busy ordering food and sipping wine. After the appetizers, she had lobster and shrimp bisque and then the classic Caesar salad. The entree consisted of tournedos and filet mignon with a cardamom velvet cream sauce. Arif would really have liked to sample the New Zealand rack of baby lamb, but reluctantly ordered the seasonal vegetables at half the price. He was continuously amazed at the amount of food that tiny woman could consume. But the gorging was not done until she devoured the most pricy desert on the menu: the chocolate Truffette de France with Valrhona white chocolate mousse. In his mind, he compiled the items' costs, trying to figure out if his checking account balance would be enough for the final tab. He thought that it would be a victory if he could avoid washing the restaurant's dishes that evening! At last, the dinner ended and he managed to cover the bill. Arif's short relationship with Vivian also ended that night. His entire month's grocery budget was wiped out in one evening.

"Will you please autograph my book?" He was once again brought back to 2015 by that unmistakable squeaky voice.

"Of course, I remember you." *How can I forget you? Thanks to you, I spent a month alternating between fasting and eating chickpeas and bread!*

But he simply signed her copy and offered her some sweets. Vivian glanced at all the delicacies spread out on the table. They represented places from around the world. There were American doughnuts and pies, beautifully decorated French pastries, Middle Eastern baklavas and halvahs and ras malai from India. Vivian's eyes widened and she wiped saliva from the corner of her mouth. Arif assumed she was about to gobble up everything like a powerful vacuum cleaner, just as she had done that evening in 1990.

To his surprise, she quickly turned around with tears in her eyes. "Thank you, but I can't have any of these sweets." She looked down at herself and sighed. "I have health issues now. I'm on a very strict diet."

Then she waved goodbye and started to trudge toward the exit. He looked at her from behind. She appeared to be dangerously overweight, and seemed to have difficulty walking. Arif felt a brief pang of pity, thinking, "*Wow, all those years of free food have really taken a toll on her!*"

All at once, he remembered a childhood trip to the zoo with his father. They had watched a baby elephant waddling around. Afterward, he had spent the entire evening giggling and mimicking the elephant's walk.

Suddenly, all of those twenty years of anger and distress caused by that horrible night long ago disappeared from his mind as he looked up at the sky through the glass ceiling, and to everyone's surprise, he bellowed, "Thank you, Food God! Finally justice is done."

# THE SCAR

Upon rising every morning, I get ready with my eyes almost closed. I comb my hair and brush my teeth squinting through eyelids opened a tiny slit just to avoid stumbling. These morning rituals are done in front of a mirror, which I avoid looking into at all costs. I learned long ago that I don't like the image staring back at me. No, I'm not a wrinkled old lady. In fact, I'm thirty-six years old. I have very fair skin, large, steel-grey eyes, a rather pointed nose, and jet-black hair which cascades down my back. My height is five feet three inches and I usually weigh around one hundred twenty pounds. Keeping physically fit is important to me, and I practice yoga religiously. I don't sound too shabby, right? Some might even say I sound *beautiful*. So why don't I like to view my face in a mirror? The answer is a huge, hideous scar across my right cheek, which makes a jagged, raised half circle extending from under the eye to beneath my right ear.

I was not born with this scar. When I was five years old, my family went on vacation to a popular mountain resort. We stayed in a lovely cottage, overlooking a fertile valley. While hiking one morning, I slipped and fell down from a slight incline and gashed my face on the edge of a sharp rock. Frantically, my parents rushed me to a local hospital. This was a small town and the doctor did a mediocre job of stitching the wound and it was infected within a few days. It took weeks to fully heal, and left behind a disfiguring scar.

My life was never the same after that. From kindergarten on, my peers teased and taunted me about my scar. *Ugly duckling. Scar face. Frankenstein.* As I got older, I started to fight back and often ended up in the principal's office. The world was unbearably cruel. Every day I would come home crying, and tears stained my pillow at night. I had a recurring nightmare that I looked in the mirror and the scar had spread all over my face. I would wake from this dream covered in sweat. Other nights, I'd dream of it magically vanishing. This dream was almost worse because she had to wake up to her sad reality.

Gradually, I became an introvert. Staying inside my room reading books about animals became my escape. I imagined that the claws of a tiger or the teeth of a shark would hurt less and heal more quickly than the emotional pain caused by human words. One day, I read about Islam, and thought about converting just so that I could hide my scar behind a burqa. However, I stopped doing that because of my religion's history. Hundreds of years ago my ancestors immigrated to India from Iran to avoid religious persecution. We are called Parsi.

I vividly recall the lowest point in my life. I was in my room, doing homework. My door was open a little, and the conversation from my parents' room drifted down the hallway.

"Our daughter is now a grown woman," I heard my mother say, "Who will ever marry her? We are going to have to offer a large dowry."

The realization hit my guts like a cricket bat. I looked in the mirror. I hadn't been imagining it after all. I was truly hideous. Someone would have to be coerced to marry me.

I sat on my bed, tears streaming over my revolting scar. I told myself I should end my own pain and stop inconveniencing my family in the process. What did I have to live for? I slipped down to the kitchen and found the jug of kerosene. I put the jug on the kitchen floor and began looking through drawers for the box of matches. I was weeping and my hands were shaking.

Suddenly, my brother's hand appeared on my arm. "I heard you banging around down here," he said. I gasped, startled. I hadn't heard him come down the stairs. "Don't be dumb, sis," he said softly. "Life is a gift not meant to be wasted at such a young age. There are people that love you." He gently took the kerosene and box of matches out of my hand and put them away. "I love you, sis." He didn't say a word to my parents.

When I was thirty, I began an arranged marriage. Initially, he was quite cordial to me, and everything seemed to be going smoothly. Looking back, I realize that our marriage was fueled by my self-sacrifice and willingness to constantly compromise.

Discovering I was pregnant was the first spark of hope I had felt in years. As my son grew in my belly, I found meaning in life. When it was time, we rushed to the hospital. Everything went smoothly. Afterward, groggy from the medication and fatigue, I drifted in and out of sleep. I opened my eyes a tiny bit to see my sweet beautiful baby boy in the bassinet right beside me. *Raj.* Then my eyes closed again. Two nurses came in and bustled around the room, thinking I was asleep.

"Cute little boy," said one.

"He sure is," agreed the other. "Good thing that huge disgusting scar didn't get passed down from mother to child."

The nurses laughed scornfully as they moved on to the next room.

I was so hurt by such an idiotic remark. I wanted to cry out that I wasn't born with a scar and that it's definitely not genetic. Unbelievably, over the years, I would hear similar comments from relatives and friends.

Raj was my pride and joy. He was clearly intelligent, and held an aptitude for music, particularly the drums. I cajoled Ajit into getting him a drum set for his birthday, and he spent hours practicing.

One day, I approached my husband with an idea. "Ajit," I said, "Raj needs an extracurricular activity. He is so good at the drums. Why don't we get him lessons?"

"Music lessons?" Ajit snapped, "No, he will join the soccer team. That will build him up physically. Make him strong. He'll love it."

"But, he's never played soccer before," I argued. "We know for certain that he likes the drums. We should nurture his interests instead of trying to decide for him."

My husband recoiled in surprise. I never stood up for myself. His lip curled. "You think you're smarter than me? A better parent than me? You're nothing."

"I'm just trying to do what's best for our son," I retorted.

"You're an airhead with silly dreams, and I'll be damned if you turn our son into some sort of weak, artistic fool who can't get a job." His face was getting red. "You're lucky your family offered such a big dowry, or you wouldn't have a husband or a son at all." I gasped, then walked away quickly to hide my pain.

Again that night, the pillow was soaked by my tears. My mind drifted back to that night in the kitchen. No brother to stop me this time. But the thought of a motherless Raj prevented me from any action. He had become my universe.

Raj continued to grow and thrive. When he was in kindergarten, his elementary school sponsored a talent contest. The idea behind this event was threefold. It would be a great way to showcase students, help build their confidence, and bring the community together. The school had students and teachers paint a bright, eclectic backdrop for the auditorium stage. The stage itself was bare, since students would provide their own props and instruments. A recently installed sound system with microphones would help to clearly hear the contestants. The children had to provide the organizers with their planned songs, music, jokes and a sundry other details of their performances. Raj was anxious to show off his new mastery of the drums. His classmate and best friend Nina would be singing her favorite song.

When the day of the contest arrived, I quickly found an empty seat in the auditorium. From the corner of my eye, I noticed a woman from my neighborhood approaching my aisle. I loathed this woman because she always managed to somehow include my scar in any conversation. Even though I pretended not to see her, by hiding my face behind the program of tonight's events, she sat down next to me and loudly announced, "Hi. Do you remember me? We've talked at other school functions." I nodded my head and pretended to be busy checking my email on my phone, but she continued to talk. Since I was fairly non-communicative, she kept asking me questions.

I simply replied, "Fine", "Okay", and "Not bad".

She finally got to the real reason she had come over to talk to me. "I have been thinking of you, my dear friend". *Friend? I don't even know your last name.* "I mentioned your scar to my nephew in America. He's a prominent doctor there. He told me that they can perform some kind of plastic surgery to fix nasty scars like you have on your face." She stopped to see my reaction, but I didn't say a word. Therefore, she continued, "The doctors in America are very expensive, though, so I doubt that you can afford their services." I finally looked up at her in disbelief. *My scar has no detrimental impact on my health,* I said inside my head. *You, on the other hand, are so overweight you can barely walk. You need to travel to America for a gastric bypass operation. You are a mean fool.* However, without saying a word aloud, I got up and found another seat.

The talent show was wonderful. The children all performed with only minor mishaps. I was particularly impressed by Raj's classmate Kalpna's gymnastic abilities and little Nina's rendition of a popular Bollywood movie song. Of course, Raj's drum solo was the best that I had ever heard him play. At the end, the audience gave all of the contestants a standing ovation.

"Okay, okay, folks. Let's calm down," the MC laughed into the microphone. The crowd settled.

"They did an amazing job, didn't they?" he asked. The audience clapped again. "Now, I have the envelope here with the judges' decision." He opened it with a flourish.

The crowd went silent. The MC cleared his throat. "Our third-place winner is...Sam, for his juggling performance!" There was applause and hoots as he came to the stage to accept the prize. "In second place...our little Bollywood star, Nina! Let's give her a hand!" Nina smiled and waved on her way up. "And finally, the first place prize for our talent show–Raj! That young man can really drum!"

The audience cheered as Raj carefully made his way over to the MC. Raj shook his hand and took the gold plaque. But suddenly, Raj saw a bouquet of roses lying on a nearby table. Quickly, he grabbed the flowers.

Rather surprised with Raj's action, the MC asked him, "Very well, sir, you can have these beautiful flowers, as long as you tell me what you are going to do with them."

Immediately, Raj replied, "I'll give them to a beautiful girl."

The audience began to laugh and clap. With a smile, the MC said, "Go ahead, young man. Let's see who that lucky girl is." Raj started to look around at the rows of faces. I could see Nina sitting quietly, smiling at him. The announcer joked, "Welcome to 2019. I started dating in high school. But now it seems everything starts very early. He's looking for his little sweetheart."

Finally, Raj's eyes settled on his honoree. He tightly held the bouquet of flowers and ran across the stage. Raj jumped from the edge of the stage, tumbled a little bit, but kept his balance. He then proceeded to the intended row and seat. While his microphone was still attached on his chest, he presented the bouquet. Happily and lovingly he said,

"These are for you, Mom. You are the most beautiful person in this world."

For the first time, my tears expressed joy as they drenched the roses.

# VELCRO

At work, Steve was very easy-going. He worked hard Monday through Friday. If his boss asked him to work overtime, he did so without complaining. If they were rearranging the office space and told him they needed to move his cubicle to the other corner, he smiled and began packing up his desk. He didn't seem picky about anything. But after Steve got home, all of that changed. Once he walked through his door, everything was exactly the way he wanted it.

Steve lived by himself, and his house was a temple of sports. He had an elaborate, high-end entertainment system and a full sports subscription package so that he could experience each televised game fully. He was very particular and had his game-spectating experience exactly the way he wanted it.

He also attended every local live game he possibly could. He often poured over sports schedules, trying to fit as many as he could into each season.

His passion included not only football, baseball, and basketball, but a multitude of other sports. His walls were densely covered with pendants and posters of teams and players from far and wide. It didn't matter if it was men's or women's, contact or non-contact, college or professional. He knew everything about every sport from lacrosse to bowling and thoroughly enjoyed all of them. But he delighted in them without interruptions.... and that meant alone! This was the problem.

Steve had a loud and boisterous coworker, Bob, who also loved sports and tended to accompany him to games without an invitation. At other times, Bob had tickets of his own, and would implore Steve to attend the event with him. Try as he might, Steve could not avoid Bob, meaning that he was usually subjected to spilled popcorn, or beer or even an annoying bop on the head from a spongy "#1" souvenir.

Steve had used every excuse to escape him, but somehow Bob continuously seemed to know his plans. You would think that with all the sports in the universe, this would be an impossibility, but Bob was always ready to go, or even waiting for his "pal" at an event. Bob would appear at Steve's side as he poured his morning coffee in the office break room, as he ate lunch in the cafeteria, and as he was enjoying a beer at a nearby sports bar after work.

One day while Steve was busy in his cubicle, his boss, Mr. Wills, stopped to talk. Mr. Wills was a friendly man and a good boss, but his idea of "sport" was the occasional game of croquet at a summer barbecue.

"Steve, your hard work has positively impacted our company's sales," Mr. Wills said enthusiastically. "I really appreciate your effort."

"Well, thank you for the feedback, sir," Steve replied. "It is nice to hear it is paying off."

"Say, Steve," Mr. Wills continued, "Do you have plans tonight? My wife and I have seats at the opera and we'd love it if you would come."

There was a local wrestling match that evening that Steve had his eye on, but Bob had already come to his desk and asked if he was going. Suddenly, Steve remembered something. *Bob hated opera!* Steve recalled Bob coming across some famous aria when scanning through the stations on his car radio. Bob had paused and done a sarcastic imitation of an opera singer, eyes to the ceiling and one hand pressed dramatically to his chest. Then he had changed the station, shaking his head and grimacing. If Steve went with Mr. Wills, there would be absolutely no chance that he would turn around and find Bob at his elbow. A Bob-free evening. Happily, Steve replied, "I would love to accompany you."

That night was magical for Steve. He was enamored with the theater as soon as he went up the magnificent polished marble steps, through the towering Corinthian columns and into the soaring, ornate atrium. His walked across the expanse of lush, richly colored carpet as his eyes traced the glittering chandeliers and brocade wallpaper. All around him, people rustled by in formal attire– tailored tuxedos and lustrous evening gowns. Then the house lights went down and the curtain came up. The costumes, the set, the soaring voices! The opera was a grand experience. Steve was reluctant to leave his seat at intermission. Nevertheless, he and Mr. Wills headed down a spiral staircase for a cocktail. They chatted and sipped their drinks, and Steve's mind wandered. He kept thinking how pleasant this evening had been without Bob's constant interference and annoying banter. He contemplated investing in season seats for the opera. Maybe a membership! He'd have to ask Mr. Wills what he thought.

Suddenly, his reverie ended as he realized that Mr. Wills was speaking to him. "I know that you are enjoying tonight by the look on your face. Many people savor some of this ambience at sports events also. I have two season tickets to a skybox at Neyland Stadium. You'd really enjoy the skybox. Privacy during the games, gourmet food, and excellent service. It is quite an experience. My wife and I are planning to spend the winter in the Bahamas, so I'll give you one of our seats as a thank-you for all your hard work, if you'd like it. I intend to give the other seat to my brother-in-law. You know him."

Steve couldn't believe his ears. He had the chance for more of this luxury combined with his beloved sports. But the best part was knowing that there would be no Bob! Steve had met the brother of Mrs. Wills, Joe, a few years ago at a Christmas party, and the two of them had immediately liked each other. As a matter of fact, he vividly remembered passionately discussing upcoming  the Redskins-versus-Eagles game with John that night.

"Mr. Wills," Steve said. "I don't know what to say. That sounds amazing. Thank you!" He was absolutely thrilled.

He was so excited, he had trouble falling asleep the entire week leading up to the first game that Sunday. On that day, he got up at dawn, showered, shaved, and listened to all of the analysts discuss the upcoming game. He dressed in his favorite team jersey and anxiously headed towards the stadium. Upon his arrival, he was amazed with the luxurious environment of the skybox. There were private ushers, food and beverage servers with an unlimited supply of delicious food, beer and wine. Steve stood there admiring the colossal stadium with an ice-cold beer in his hand while he waited for Mr. Wills' brother-in law, Joe to appear.

"Hi, Steviemyboy."

Steve flinched. That voice. There was only one person that could be. His knees buckled, and he broke into a cold sweat as he turned around to face Bob standing before him!

"Bob? What the heck are you doing here?"

"What do you mean? Didn't Mr. Wills tell you that I will be joining you to watch all the games for the rest of the season?"

"No. He told me his brother in-law would accompany me. So I was expecting Joe."

"Relax, Steve. I know way more about football than Joe. Didn't you know my wife is Mr. Will's sister? Small world, huh? You and I will have so much fun this whole season!"

Well, Steve got his seat at the luxury Skybox, but he also got Bob with all his irksome habits. Yes, he definitely is still stuck to him like Velcro!

# THE GOALS

The elevator doors opened. Amy emerged and dragged her two suitcases across the lobby, erupting through the front doors of the Palazzo Navona hotel. Then she stopped short, frozen on a busy sidewalk of Rome. She had no idea what to do next.

All her thirty years of life, mother and father made all the decisions for her. Mom picked out all her dresses and told her what to do next on every occasion. Dad arranged all of her activities and trips. She was an only child and had very protective parents. As she got older, her "manager" became her boyfriend, Mike. He had arranged this trip. For the last five days, she was just following him around Rome. He planned all the activities and sightseeing trips to visit monuments and museums. For breakfast, lunch, and dinner, he would decide which restaurants they enjoyed, even ordering her food. It made her feel loved that he knew what she would like to eat and more importantly, what she would not like. But all of that had crumbled in a single moment. Now she was standing all alone on the busy street in front of Palazzo Navona.

It was one of the most beautiful and picturesque areas of Rome. Throngs of people were hanging out in cafés, boutiques, art galleries, and wine bars. Endless museums and monuments were within walking distance. The streets were busy with swerving bicyclists and chic Italians on Vespas. Street vendors, merchants, and locals were roaming around in a noisy cacophony of life in Rome. There was no rhyme or reason to the winding streets and there was something to see around every corner. Normally this carnival of culture would be delightful, but today it only added to her sense of chaos and upheaval. She didn't know what to do and where to go next. She knew her return ticket to New York was from Venice, but she had no clue how to get to Venice. Suddenly, Amy had to make decisions.

As she was lost in thought, a car with four young men stopped in front of her. One of them yelled at her in an Italian accent, "Hey baby, do you want to come with us?" Other guys in the car laughed and all of a sudden Amy realized how vulnerable she is in a foreign country. Tears came out of nowhere, and her face burned with embarrassment as the men screeched away, laughing. Gathering her wits, she started looking around and recognized a nearby café where she and Mike had gone every morning that week for cappuccino. Quickly, she dragged both suitcases into the cafe. She sat at their favorite table near the window.

"Buongiorno. Good morning, Madam." A familiar voice calmed her down.

"Hello," she said with a smile. "The usual, please."

Maria, her server was a middle-aged lady, fluent in English and Italian. She brought two cappuccinos and pastries, assuming Mike would be joining soon. After finishing both cappuccinos, Amy asked Maria how she can get to Venice from Rome.

"Ah, by train." Maria replied. "Italian trains are very comfortable and fast."

"Um, where is the train station?" asked Amy nervously.

"The quickest way to go to Roma Termini from here is to take a taxi. You can get one for ten euros. It will get you there in four minutes."

After paying a bill and hugging Maria for last five days excellent service, Amy hailed a taxi.

Amy was mesmerized entering the train station's lobby hall, a tall space of monumental dimensions. The great hall was fronted by full-height glass walls and was covered with a concrete roof that consisted of a flattened segmented arch, a modernist version of a barrel vault from ancient Roman architecture. The vault was structurally integrated with a cantilevered canopy that extended over the entrance portico. The end result was a gravity-defying modernist structure. The back of the hall led to a transition space for ticketing before reaching the train bays and was topped by an even longer building connecting to a ten-story hotel.

"I need to get to Venice, please."

"You have two choices," explained the frail-looking, silver-haired man behind the ticket counter. "You can take the high-speed train from Rome to Venice. It is a modern and luxurious train will get you to your destination in only three hours and seven minutes. And it costs eleven euros one way. Or you can take the train which stops in Florence and then goes to Venice."

"Which one leaves first?" she questioned.

"Well, train to Florence leaves in about five minutes from track number nine."

"I'll take that one. First-class please." Amy quickly responded. *The sooner she was out of Rome, the better*, she thought.

Amy ran to catch the train. After settling down in her designated seat, she looked at her phone. She heard another text alert. *Mike.* She didn't want to look at them till she was well on her way. As soon as the train departed Rome, Amy looked at the messages. All were from Mike.

*I'm sorry.*
*Please call me.*
*I'm worried about you.*
*I love you.*
*I miss you.*

Looking at Mike's picture affixed to the messages, Amy started to cry. Tears fell on the phone. She pulled out a tiny handkerchief to wipe the phone and started to talk to herself. "If you love me then why did you do that, Mikey? Do you have any idea how much it hurt me?"

"Hello? Are you alright?" asked a sweet, comforting voice. A middle-aged woman was sitting across from Amy. Up until now, Amy was busy putting suitcases away properly and checking her phone that she didn't even notice the other passenger seated across from her in the train car.

"Hi, my name is Sofia."

"I'm Amy."

"American?"

"Yes, how did you know?"

"Your T-shirt told me." They laughed at the same time. Amy was wearing San Francisco 49ers T-shirt.

"And you are? British?" guessed Amy.

"No, Italian. But I studied at Oxford. Did you have fun in Roma?" Sofia asked.

"Oh, yes!" Amy enthusiastically recounted seeing the Colosseum, St. Peter's Square and Basilica, The Pantheon, Trevi Fountain, Spanish Steps, and, of course, the Vatican.

"Good. Did you throw a coin in the fountain at Spanish steps and make a wish?"

"Yes, I wished that I can achieve all my goals in life."

"Ah, goals. That is a whole day's conversation in itself, no?" Sofia smiled. "How about food? Did you enjoy our cappuccino?"

"Of course. We loved having cappuccino and pastries in cafes the most."

"We?"

"Mike, my...boyfriend."

"And where is he?"

Amy paused, but something in Sofia's face made her continue.

"We had such a great time during the last five days in Rome," Amy said, staring out of the window. "Yesterday was our last day, so we went to a very nice club to go dancing. We danced for hours, and were about to leave. When I came back from the restroom, I saw Mike laughing with some Italian girls. One of them was holding his hand." Amy stopped and blinked back tears. "I got so angry at him and couldn't sleep the whole night. We started fighting about it and he told me those Italian girls didn't mean anything to him, and he loved only me and he had been planning to propose to me in Venice during a gondola ride tonight." She shook her head and continued, "He is the only guy I have dated. It's been ten years."

Sofia seemed to be thinking. "Tell me more about Mike. How did you meet? What is he like when he's not being a scoundrel?" She smiled a little.

"He is a handsome man with thick curly hair and a loving smile." Amy closed her eyes and smiled. "A very kind man, never loses temper. I met him when I was a sophomore. It was a love at first sight. We were inseparable. My parents loved him too. After graduation we both worked for the same company for eight years and now planning to start our own business. We both are career-oriented and work very hard to achieve our goals."

"Any plans to get married and start a family?" Sofia prodded.

"Marriage, yes, no thoughts about starting a family. Lots of goals and dreams to fulfill before that." But then with a sigh, she quickly added, "Now I don't know what to do. I'm so confused. He has never cheated on me, though." Again, tears came to her eyes.

Sofia handed her a paper napkin to dry her eyes and said, "You know what I think? Never judge a person from one incident. Always look at the overall picture. Maybe he was just kidding around with those girls. Maybe those girls were flirting with him. Young Italian girls love to come on to tourists. Or maybe he had too much wine that night. I bet he'll never do it again."

Amy's head swam in confusion. The memory of Mike smiling at that girl made her blood boil, but she knew he wasn't that kind of guy. And there was so much that was good about him. She could think of no one else she would rather spend her life with. She knew in that moment that she could forgive him. This realization was followed by a rush of panic. She was on a *train*! Headed for the *airport*! Going to *Venice*! Without Mike! What had she done? She pulled out her phone and began typing frantically. Seconds later, she heard a *ding*. A message from Mike.

"I wasn't going to let you walk away without saying I'm sorry one more time. Maria, the server at our favorite café told me where you went. I'm already boarding a plane, heading for Venice. I'll be waiting for you at the train station with a dozen roses. Love you."

"Oh my god! Mikey is flying to Venice." Amy squealed with joy. Immediately she replied, "My train is arriving Venice 4:30pm. Love you too."

"Ah, see? A happy ending. Time to celebrate!" Sofia waved over a server and rattled off a long order in Italian.

"It sounds like you ordered the whole menu!" exclaimed Amy.

"To share with my friend, no?" replied Sofia.

A moment later, the server brought a bottle of Sassicaia and cheese from the Tuscany region.

"Cheers!" Sofia raised the glass. "Or shall we say 'Saluti'?"

They sipped together. "Wow!" Amy exclaimed. Sofia peered at her over her glass.

"Yes, this is a good one. You have a refined palate. I know this wine well. An elegant full-bodied wine with aromas of red berry, blue flower, menthol, exotic spices and a whiff of French oak which takes shape on this impeccably balanced radiant red. The palate is vibrant and focused – almost ethereal–delivering raspberry compote, Marasca cherry, and cinnamon in elegant tannins." She sighed blissfully and took another sip.

Impressed with that description, Amy questioned, "Who are you? A wine connoisseur?"

"I own a winery in Tuscany." Sofia pulled an iPad out of her bag and tapped the screen, showing Amy a picture of a beautiful winery and a gorgeous farmhouse.

"Oh my god. Do you really own a winery?" gushed Amy. "That is my biggest dream. The goal of my life. I grew up thirty miles from Napa Valley."

Next, the server brought two cappuccinos and a tray of *dolci*. The tray had five of the most popular Italian sweets: Gelato, Cannoli, Panettone, Sfogliatelle, and Tiramisu—Italy's most famous dessert.

A silence fell over the compartment as they slowly enjoyed the food. Through the windows, row after row of grapevines rushed by.

"Amy, listen to me," Sofia said suddenly. "Sometimes in life, while chasing "big" goals, we either ignore or postpone very *important* goals. In the end, those goals matter the most in life but then it's too late to achieve them." She paused as her voice got choked up but she continued. "If you aren't careful, you could end up living with emptiness for the rest of your life."

"Ladies and Gentlemen, we will be arriving at Santa Maria Novella station in Florence, in ten minutes," the announcement interrupted their conversation. "Thank you for traveling with us. Have a wonderful time in Florence."

Sofia wiped her eyes, pulled out one old paper from her purse and handed it to Amy. The train was beginning to slow as it approached the station.

"Darling, at your age I also had a goal list. I almost achieved all of them but missed out on number five. Do me a favor, in your life when you fulfill this goal, please send this paper back to me?"

Amy looked at the list. *Graduate from High School with all As, get an undergraduate degree in Science from Italy's most prestigious college, go to England and get a Ph.D. in Chemistry from Oxford, own a beautiful winery in Tuscany,* and the list continued. All goals were marked "Done" except number five.

They swayed a bit as the train came to a halt. The speaker announced their arrival in Florence. Sofia got up, hugged Amy and left. Amy sat, lost in thought until the train started moving again. She couldn't wait to see Mike.

*Florence, Italy, two years later.*
"Madam, mail."

A maid put a stack of mail on Sofia's desk. After going through some business mail, she noticed an envelope with a handwritten address. It was from San Francisco. Curiously, she opened it. There was a picture of a woman holding a baby. Looking at the woman's face she remembered the American girl she met on the train to Florence. In addition to that picture, she found a wrinkled-up, yellowed paper in the envelope. As Sofia was unfolding the paper, she thought *"Maybe Amy bought a winery. So soon?"* But the handwriting seemed to be very familiar to her.

"Oh my god, it's my old goal list," she exclaimed in disbelief.

Quickly she looked down the list. The number five goal: *Be a mother before it's too late*, was scratched out, and marked with a note: "DONE."

Sofia sat and stared at the photo again. Underneath the picture it was written "Amy & Sofia."

She clenched the note and soaked the paper with tears of joy.

# AMERICAN GANDHI

"Ladies and gentlemen, we will soon be landing at Washington National Airport. Sit back, relax and enjoy the rest of the flight," announced the Pan Am pilot.

My heart started to pound with excitement. I was traveling from India to the United States of America to continue my studies in engineering. At the gate, Mr. Thomas, my student advisor, greeted me with an enthusiastic "Welcome to America!" He was wearing gold-framed glasses and had long sideburns. He drove me to the George Washington University campus. After climbing two floors, we knocked at room 222. A skinny guy wearing thick glasses opened the door. Mr. Thomas introduced me to Leon, who would be my roommate for the rest of my college years.

In the next few days, Leon and I became good friends. I often saw him reading Mahatma Gandhi's *Experiments of Truth* book. He believed and followed Gandhi's principles of nonviolence and the ethic of refraining from lying. He was a shy guy who didn't have much interest in sports, except swimming. Every Saturday morning he attended a swimming class.

After one month at school, I was approached by a tall, muscular guy.

"Hey, buddy. I'm Joe and I play point guard for the school's basketball team. I need your help."

"What kind of help?" I asked.

"I'm struggling in my calculus class. I want you to help me with some of my assignments." Although he was polite, it sounded more like an order, rather than a request. My first inclination was to decline; however, his intimidating size changed my mind. Then Joe added, "During basketball season, I will make sure you get a front-row seat at mid-court." He pulled out a paper napkin, scribbled his name, and wrote "Give a big frosty one to my Indian friend." Handing me the note, he instructed, "Go to Bob's bar near DuPont circle and give this to the bartender named Alice. She is my babe."

One hot afternoon, after a stressful class, I walked into that bar. It looked like a saloon from an old Western movie. There were a few barstools, some chairs and broken wooden benches. It was 1968 and graffiti was all over the walls, advocating both for and against the Vietnam War. Behind the counter, I saw a tall, beautiful girl with a pierced nose and long hair reaching down to her hips. She was adeptly pouring beer and mixing cocktails for several customers at once.

Sitting down on a bar stool, I greeted her. "Hi, I'm a friend of Joe."

She responded, "Hello. I'm Alice. What can I get you?"

I gave her the note from Joe. She smiled and poured a cold beer from the tap. While she was pouring the beer, my eyes slid down to her cleavage. There was a beautiful tattoo of a lovebird on her left breast. The bird's head was red, chest was yellow, feathers were olive green and tiny beak was yellow. Alluring combination of colors and monochromatic shading created a superb lovebird tattoo.

"Do you like it?"

I glanced up and realized she had seen me looking.

"Yes," I stuttered, blushing. "I like the bird, I mean."

"That's what they all say." She winked and handed me the beer. While wiping some stains from the counter, she explained that the bird is a symbol for freedom. "Birds can walk on the earth and swim in the water as humans do, but they also have the ability to fly in the air. They are free to roam the earth as well as the sky. They symbolize eternal life, the link between earth and heaven. I believe tattoos should be symbols of ideas you like: for me it is love, peace and hope."

After a few sips of beer, I started to get a headache. Puzzled, I asked her, "Why does my head hurt already? Is this a very strong beer?"

She laughed and told me to look around the room. I turned and saw many young long-haired, bearded men smoking. It hung thickly in the air like fog. "That's the stuff giving you a headache. It's called 'pot.'" Then she paused and asked me, "How come you don't know about pot? Aren't you from India? Didn't the Beatles go there to smoke?"

"Not really. They went there for the music. Although I am from India, my parents were very protective. Growing up there was no beer, no drugs, not even cigarettes."

She laughed. "Well, welcome to America, then."

I said nothing for a while and kept sipping beer. My mind was overflowing with questions. Usually, lovebirds are depicted as a pair. In nature, they do not survive without each other. She must have another tattoo of a lovebird on her body. I didn't see it. So where was that other tattoo?

"You're wondering where the other love bird is, aren't you?" I glanced up and saw a knowing expression on her lovely face.

I hate when people read me like that.

"Are you going to tell me?" I asked, trying to seem confident.

"Ha-ha. Everyone in this town wants to know the answer to that." She left me to serve others.

I finished my beer, left her a tip and walked out.

When I reached my room, I saw Leon reading an autobiography of Gandhi. I told him all about meeting Alice in the bar and said, "Love birds always come in a pair. So I wonder where on her body the other tattoo is."

Leon smiled and said, "Actually, I know where it is."

I jumped from my bed yelling, "What? Listen to me, Leon. I hope you don't know that. And even if you do, please don't you ever tell that to anyone. Have you seen the size of her boyfriend Joe and his buddies?"

Leon calmly turned the lights off and said, "You know damn well that I don't lie. Good night!"

The next morning, Leon was sitting at the kitchen table when I came out for breakfast. I filled the coffeemaker with water and scooped coffee from the canister into the filter.

"When I was eight years old, I broke a beautiful vase at home," said Leon, suddenly breaking the silence. "It was my Dad's favorite. He got it from Amsterdam. I was scared and lied to him by saying that our cat broke it. At bedtime he asked me three times 'Are you sure the cat did it?' But once you lie, you have to stick to your story. The next morning Dad brought me Mahatma Gandhi's autobiography and told me "Son, every religion in the world condemns lying. When you lie to someone you lie to yourself, and you have to live with it forever. Read this book and you will learn some very important lessons in life.' I hugged him, and with tears in my eyes, confessed my lie. From that day onwards I have never lied."

Weeks quickly passed. I got busy with studying and forgot my conversation with Leon about Alice's tattoo. I stopped by the bar on a different night, but Alice wasn't working.

One Friday evening Leon and I invited a few students to our room for a game of poker. We were all laughing, joking, and drinking beer while we played cards. All of a sudden, the topic of tattoos came up.

"Best-tattoo-on-a-woman award goes to that gorgeous bartender over at Bob's," one of the guys said. "The one that's dating that jock? She's got that lovebird..." He fanned his face and shook his head and everyone laughed.

"Alice," said someone else. "She's in one of my classes. She's really nice—and smart."

"I know her boyfriend, Joe," said another. "Trust me. No one else knows the location of the second tattoo except him." Everyone laughed. Leon opened his third beer and took a big gulp. Since two beers was his limit, I became concerned about what might come out of his mouth next. Then with a big smile he said, "I know the site of the other tattoo."

Instantly, everyone fell silent.

"What?"

"You know? How can a nerdy kid like you know such a secret?"

"No freaking way." Everyone was staring at him.

"Well, where is it?"

Before I could stop him, Leon declared, "The famous tattoo is four inches down her right thigh."

There was a silence so heavy that you could hear a pin drop. I screamed, "He is drunk. He doesn't know what he is saying. The party is over." I abruptly kicked everyone out.

After putting away the poker chips and throwing empty beer cans in the trash, I said to Leon, "You made the biggest mistake of your life tonight. Tomorrow morning you must tell everyone that you got so drunk that you were making things up."

For the first time, Leon raised his voice, pointed his finger towards me and yelled, "I never lie." That night I lay awake worrying about Leon's safety.

The next morning, I heard someone knocking on our door. Before I could get up, the door was knocked down from its hinges by a big kick. Joe jumped up onto Leon's bed and stood over him. Three scary guys stood around the bed, waiting. He lifted Leon from his bed, slapping his face, growling, "You are a liar! I heard you were saying some things about my girl's tattoo last night."

Leon's lip was bleeding, but he still managed to mumble, "I never lie."

I lay in bed trying not to breathe. I wished I could spring up and execute a burst of karate moves, fighting off my friend's attackers like a hero in a Bollywood movie, but I could not.

Joe cocked his fist towards Leon's face and screamed, "You son of a bitch. If you aren't lying then tell me right now, how do you know where the second bird is? I swear I will kill you!" I saw nothing but rage in his eyes. I knew that he wasn't bluffing. Even though Joe still had him by the collar, Leon quietly reached down and picked up his broken glasses from the bed and wiped his bloody face with his sleeve. Joe stared at him, his fist ready. I closed my eyes and started to pray to all the gods of the universe. Joe launched his fist. Leon spoke.

"I know it because she is in my swimming class."

Joe's fist stopped just a fraction of an inch from Leon's head.

# THE SEVENTH STAR

Kumar opened his eyes and smiled. "Another day, how wonderful!" Every night before he went to bed, a final thought in his mind was, "Did I live today to the fullest? It could be my last."

Ever since his friend, Bob, died in his sleep, he was keenly aware that the same thing could happen to him. Kumar would rather pass away like his buddy, Don, who loved hiking, and met his demise climbing the Himalayas. *What a way to go– doing your favorite thing,* he thought.

He got out of bed while everyone in the house was still sleeping. Without making a noise, he brewed some fragrant masala tea and took it to the three-season porch at the back of the house, his favorite place in his daughter Sonal's home. She had insisted he move in with her after his wife passed away. He had a one granddaughter named Smita, who was the center of his universe.

The view from the porch was a gorgeous vista—a large oval-shaped pond frequented by ducks and a thick stand of trees that harbored a variety of birds. Kumar had tempted the birds closer to the house with a bird house that he had built and put on a post nearby. He spent hours in contemplation on that porch, gazing at the perpetual ballet of nature. On gloomy mornings, he sipped steaming tea while watching raindrops falling on the water. In the afternoons he sat, reading books and napping. By late evening, he would sneak a few sips of his favorite single malt whiskey as he watched the sky flush crimson. Kumar was a retired scientist who had worked many years for NASA.

"Come in and get ready, Dad," He heard his daughter say. "Remember you have a doctor's appointment at ten o'clock." Kumar had grudgingly agreed to see a lung specialist.

After navigating through midmorning Columbus traffic, they arrived at the doctor's clinic.

A nurse led him to an examination room. After taking his pulse and blood pressure, she left him in the room and told him that the doctor would see him soon. *Yeah right. Forty minutes if I'm lucky*, he thought.

As he sat on a chair, he looked around the room. On one side was a high exam table. A cabinet was in a far-right corner containing some gloves, masks, and cleaning agents.

The smell of a disinfectant permeated the air. On one wall he observed an eye chart and blood pressure monitor and on another wall was a comprehensive anatomy poster. After looking at the walls he mumbled, "How gross." He couldn't understand why beautiful artwork was not hung up in order to calm patients. Kumar would have liked a lovely blue sky, a gorgeous sunset, or even

meandering peaceful river on the walls. Van Gogh's
*Starry Night* would have been perfect. He picked
up a magazine and started to flip through the pages.
After a short while, he got bored and threw the
magazine down and mumbled disgust at its gossipy
content.

After a lengthy time, a man in his late fifties with
gold-framed glasses and salt-and-pepper hair
entered the room with a laptop in his hand. He
wore a white coat, and a stethoscope was hanging
from his neck. With a big smile, he greeted Kumar.
"Hello, I'm Doctor Smith. How are we doing
today?"

*Why is he using the word we? You are doing
fine Doc. I'm the one who is not.* "I'm fine."

"Okay let's have a look at you." The doctor
clicked the penlight and looked at Kumar's eyes.
"Open your mouth, please." He gently tipped the
older man's head from side to side, peeking into his
mouth with the light. With his fingertips, he felt
along the sides of his neck for anything unusual.
He pulled out his stethoscope and put the cold disk
against Kumar's chest, inside his paper drape.

"Inhale for me," he said, listening in the
earpieces. Kumar inhaled slowly, then coughed.
"Nurse?" Dr. Smith called. She appeared in
seconds. "Bring me a cup of water." She nodded
and disappeared, returning with a small plastic cup
for Kumar. Once his breathing was settled, the
doctor moved the stethoscope to the other side.
"Again, please?" Kumar took a slow breath, then
coughed again. The doctor waited patiently for him
to stop, then moved to his back, asking him to
inhale as he listened to each side.

While Kumar was putting on his clothes, Doctor
Smith left to speak to Sonal. "I am sorry to say that
his COPD is advancing. Is he using his inhaler?"

She shook her head. "He is so stubborn. He says he doesn't need it."

"His lung capacity is at forty percent," continued the doctor. "Have him keep the rescue inhaler nearby at all times, and absolutely no smoking! Try to keep him indoors during cold weather. The chances of getting pneumonia are high for a man with his condition and age. He's going to put himself in the hospital."

She sighed. "Asking him to stay inside is impossible. It would be like telling a fish to stay out of water. If you keep him away from the nature, he'll die. Sitting outside and looking at the sky is therapy for him. Although, I will make sure he isn't over-exposed to the cold." Dr. Smith furrowed his brow and nodded.

After reaching home, Kumar went to the porch to take a nap. A knock on the door woke him up. His friend, Professor Edward, was there with a book in his hand. He was teaching philosophy at Ohio State University. Kumar greeted him with a big smile. He always liked intellectual discussions with the professor. Edward handed him a book: *Origin* by Dan Brown. Kumar lifted the four-hundred-sixty-page book and immediately gave it back to Ed saying, "My friend, I have no time to read this long book. Tell me, what is it about?"

"It's a mystery novel—a thriller, but a whole lot more." The professor sat down across from Kumar. "He writes about the mysteries of life and existence. He makes his reader think about the unknown. Let me read a bit to you, just to give us something to do."

Kumar grunted noncommittally.

"'Where do we come from? Where are we going? Our origin and our destiny. These fundamental questions of human existence have always obsessed us, and for years we have dreamed of finding the answers. Where do we come from?'"

Edward looked up from the book at his friend. "Don't you agree? Every culture on Earth has a creation story. Some deity or superior being fashioning a mortal from some elemental material, infusing it with life and a will...and giving it this world to live on."

Kumar smiled. He knew his friend was trying to lead him into a philosophical discussion. This was the nature of their friendship. "Just because all of the cultures of the world believe it doesn't make it true. It just means that all people have a need to know where they came from, and in lieu of an explanation, they will invent one."

Ed shrugged and didn't offer a counter-strike. It wasn't supposed to be that kind of conversation.

"Do you ever wonder where we are going?" he asked, treading carefully around the memory of his friend's wife. "Humans throughout history certainly have. Dan Brown lists 'pristine heavens, fiery hells, hieroglyphs of the Egyptian Book of the Dead, stone carvings of astral projections...' the Greeks' Elysian fields, the Kabbalistic Gilgul neshamot, reincarnation, '...the Theosophical circles of the Summerland...'" The professor looked up from the book, marking the page with his finger.

"Yes, and, historically, when people disagree about this topic, they take it as license to kill one another," snapped Kumar. "Possibly to help their enemies see which one of them was right about the afterlife? So noble."

Edward laughed grimly. "Dan Brown would agree with you. Let me read." He flipped some pages and took a breath. "'Since the beginning of religious history, our species has been caught in a never-ending crossfire—atheists, Christians,

Muslims, Jews, Hindus, the faithful of religions—
and the only thing that unites us all is our deep
longing for peace.'"

"Bravo! This man has clearly thought about the
nature of existence extensively," Kumar said,
leaning back. "However, at this point in my life, I'm
not interested in 'Where did I come from?' I'm only
interested in 'Where am I going?'"

"So where are you going?" The professor gave
him a sly smile.

"To tell you the truth, in my opinion, either you
go six feet under or are turned into ashes. There is
no concrete evidence of anything more, my friend.
All other things are imagined by humans to give
peace to a dying person and his family," Kumar
replied.

The professor got up, patted on Kumar's
shoulder and said, "Well, thank you for a few
moments of intellectual stimulation. I can always
count on you for a counter-opinion. You're not
going anywhere soon, my friend. See you in a
couple of days." And he left.

After Ed left, Smita's head appeared around the
corner of the door. Kumar hadn't known she was
there.

"Were you listening, my little dear?" he asked.
She nodded timidly, then ran up and sat next to her
grandfather. He hoped she hadn't been frightened
by their talk of ashes and being buried in the
ground.

"Grandpa," she asked softly, "what happens after
we die?" He paused. His first instinct was to give
her the same answer he had given his friend—
nothing happens.

*How can I explain those things to such an
innocent child? She has not even lived a fraction of
this beautiful life and here I'm trying to explain*

*about the ugliness of death.* So he asked her to look through his telescope. Smita was thrilled by the sight of all those shining stars. "Wow. It's so beautiful."

Looking at her happy face, he explained, "That's your answer, dear. After someone dies, he or she turns into a lovely star." Her face lit up.

Then he asked her, "Would you like to learn more about those stars?"

"Yes, please tell me about them," she replied enthusiastically.

He asked her to look up without the telescope. "Do you see those seven bright stars?"

"Wait," she counted in a whisper under her breath, "I count six."

"Smart girl," Kumar laughed. "This is the constellation called Saptarishi–the Seven Sages. The seventh star is right there," he pointed, "hiding behind that cloud."

"Are you sure it's there?" demanded his spunky granddaughter.

"Of course I am!" Kumar said, smiling. "Now. The most famous group of stars in the Big Dipper are Alkaid, Mizar, Aloth, Megrez, Phecda, Dubhe and Merak. They are named after seven Rishis. They send energy and knowledge down to us. What do you think of that?"

But by then Smita heard Sonal calling her and she ran inside.

After Smita left, Kumar took a big sip of his favorite scotch whiskey, Glen Levitt. He looked up again and saw those seven stars. He began to silently give them names.

On the top of the rectangle, Grandpa and Grandma were chosen. He moved to the rectangle's bottom, calling those two stars Mom and Dad. His late friend Bob became the first star off the tail.

Right underneath that star, he ascribed the brightest one to his loving wife. He determined that the remaining star, the one hidden by the clouds, would someday inherit his name. He gazed at the sky, waiting for the star to show itself so that he could claim it. It remained hidden, and he smiled and whispered to himself, *Well, it seems that my turn is not tonight.*

He finished the remaining whiskey and closed his eyes. He had considered smoking a cigar, but one was not within his reach. The cool night air was beginning to settle in. He drifted peacefully in and out of consciousness. After about an hour, he woke up shivering and coughing violently. Red blood stained his shirt. As he tried to get up, his legs buckled, and he fell to the floor. He felt himself fading. *What a beautiful life this has been,* he thought.

Inside the house, Sonal had fallen asleep watching television. Suddenly, she woke up and realized that her dad was still out on the patio. Panicked, she ran outside.

Smita came out of her room and joined her worried mother. They found him motionless on the floor. Sonal picked up his hand but could not find the pulse. Crying hysterically, she dialed 911.

"Help! My dad is gone!" she sobbed.

In all the commotion, Smita suddenly noticed the most peaceful look on his face. Remembering her conversation with Grandpa, she looked up and excitedly said, "No, Mom, he's not gone. Grandpa is right there!"

She pointed upward. The clouds had moved, and the seventh star was shining.

# A DAY AT THE RACES

As the alarm clock sounded, Ravi slapped it and went back to sleep without ever opening his eyes. After a couple of hours, he rolled over with a sleepy groan and looked at his phone. The numbers in the center of his screen read 9:09 a.m. He glanced at the corner of the screen, where he saw the date was September 9. 9/9. In the year 1999.This coincidence pleased, but did not surprise him. Ravi smiled and recalled that his mother had always told him about the importance of the number nine in his life. He had been born on the Hindu religious holiday called Ram Navmi. This was the honored birthdate of Lord Rama, known as the seventh avatar of the Hindu god, Vishnu. "Navmi" means "nine" and is considered lucky. Ravi was born on the ninth day of the month.

After getting ready for the day, he went out for breakfast. He took the number nine bus to downtown Philadelphia. When he arrived at his favorite restaurant, there was a sign outside announcing a buffet breakfast for $9.99. It seemed that since waking up that morning, he kept seeing the number the number nine almost constantly.

After eating, Ravi began to stroll down the street and window shop. He stopped outside a building with an intriguing large sign in the window. It read simply, "Know Your Future Now." He looked in the open door and saw a heavyset gypsy woman sitting in an overstuffed recliner. She had long black hair and faded azure eyes which still held a twinkle. He remembered that the Gypsy tribe was originated in India. She was waving a fan that looked as if it were made of peacock feathers. Behind her was a large wooden bookcase containing many books about astrology. Speaking in a heavy European accent, she invited him inside. "Come here young man and I'll read your future for only ten dollars."

Suddenly, he burst out, "How about doing it for nine?"

She nodded and beckoned him in. He sat across from her at the table as she shuffled cards. "Take a card from me. Any card. Whatever your hand chooses." Ravi pulled one smoothly from the deck. Nine of hearts.

"Young man," she said, looking into his eyes, "So few people your age are so open, so receptive to the interconnectedness of the universe. But I can see that you are in touch with it. I see much prosperity for you with the number nine. You must take advantage of this good luck today. Go to the racetrack and bet on the number nine horse. The universe will not disappoint you." Ravi promptly paid her the nine dollars. He stepped out onto the sidewalk and searched the map app on his phone for the local race track. After walking a few blocks, he found a bank and withdrew one thousand dollars. It was then he realized that he had never been to a race track and didn't know anything about placing a bet.

This is the point in the story where my phone started to ring. "I need your help, Rajen." he implored.

"Of course, I'll help you. What's going on?" I was concerned because he was the son of a hometown family friend.

With a little hesitancy, he asked, "Can you accompany me to the racetrack today? Since you go there often, I'd like your advice on placing a bet."

"You got it, but I have some things I have to finish here first. Can you give me an hour and half?" Unbeknownst to me at the time, Ravi was pleased by the ninety-minute wait as the number nine had showed up again. Exactly ninety minutes later I picked him up and we drove to Philadelphia Park.

"There are a total of nine races today," I said, launching into my crash course on betting on horse-races as we walked along. "Each race features a random number of horses. In the first race six horses will run. The second race will have eight horses. In the thir–"

"How many horses are in the ninth race?" interrupted my friend.

After checking my guide, I answered, "Nine, why?"

He simply smiled and said, "Swell."

"Okay, moving on," I said. "Each horse is also given a name in addition to the number. Some are called Fancy Candy, Favorite Song, Hey Prince, and..."

Again, he interrupted me with a question, "What's the name of the ninth horse in the ninth race?"

I looked at my guide and answered, "Now More Than Ever."

He just grinned and patted his pocket.

"Okay, are you ready for some horse-betting vocabulary?" I asked. "Win- if your horse finishes first, you win money. Place- if your horse wins first or second, you win money. Show - if your horse finishes first, second, or third you win money." I rattled on, showing off my knowledge. "Across the board- three equal win, show, place bets. Exacta is when you choose two horses in one race. A quinella is for two horses and a trifecta for three horses in one race. Of course, your final prize is based on the winning odds for that particular horse."

I looked at him. "Are you even listening?" I demanded.

He merely tapped the wad of money stuffed in inner jacket pocket and asserted, "All I want to do is bet nine hundred ninety-nine dollars on the number nine horse in the ninth race."

"What?" I uttered, in total disbelief. "Unless you have an inside tip, that much amount of money on a single horse is unheard-of at any track!" I flipped through the guide, and as I read the analyses and my jaw dropped.

"The odds for that horse to win are seventy to one. With such a very low probability to win, you'll lose all your money." Even with my admonishment, he would not change his mind. Frustrated, I shook my head and left to get us a few beers at the bar. After I returned, I just told him to relax and wait for the ninth race. In order to take my mind off the situation, I decided to place a few bets of my own.

Apparently, after I left, Ravi decided to examine his surroundings before the ninth race. There was a beautiful oval-shaped pond surrounded by railing. It was around this that the horses raced. He enjoyed looking at the horses' manes and thick tails. They had such well-developed bodies and long, thin legs. A horse's strength was in his legs. Ravi really had admired those animals.

Meanwhile, I had begun to place bets on the other races. As usual, I would sometimes win and sometimes lose. Betting on horses is an emotional rollercoaster. As I sat there, I was laughing in victory one moment, and cursing in frustration the next. It often occurred to me that the race track, like other gambling outlets, is an intersection between the poorest and richest in society. The rich sit upstairs in their fancy boxes and the poor are downstairs on benches. The rich sip fine whiskey while eating steaks and the poor gulp beer while eating hot dogs. Even though they both bet on the same horses, the wager may greatly vary.

Finally, it was time to place a bet on the ninth race. As we walked toward the betting window, I still tried to convince Ravi that his intended bet was a huge mistake. I placed my two-dollar bet on the favored horse and then waited for Ravi. He calmly, without any hesitation, bet nine hundred ninety-nine dollars on the number nine horse to win. The young woman at the window seemed stunned with his bet, but she took the money, gave him a ticket, and with a smile, said, "Good luck."

At the sound of a bugle, the gates opened and all the horses thundered down the track. People immediately jumped from their seats and began to cheer for their selections. The jockeys in their colorful suits, stood up in the stirrups, bent forward, and used their whips to help focus the horses. A colorful commentary describing the status of each horse was being announced on the loudspeaker. Ravi's heart started to pound as he realized that Number Nine was in the lead. He sprung up screaming, "Come on, Number Nine! You can do it!" Suddenly, the momentum changed and Number Two, Number Four, and Number Five edged forward in the pack. With a burst of speed, Number Two took the lead. Before Ravi could comprehend what was happening, the race ended.

He couldn't believe the final results. Sitting down, he vigorously shook his head, while his hands grasped both sides of it. Tears rolled down his cheeks as he cried out, "It's impossible, just impossible! How could my lucky Number Nine not win?"

I was worried about him reaching a breaking point. I placed my hand on his shoulder and tried to console him by saying, "My dear friend, I'm sorry, but that's an example of how unpredictable life is. Sometimes we win, but other times we lose. Look around at these people. Most of them lost today. I don't win all the time. I just love the excitement whether that entails winning or losing. This is not for everyone, and a day at the track can be a life lesson. Let's leave and have dinner on me."

A still-shaken Ravi slowly got up from his seat. I put my arm over his shoulders to comfort him and we walked towards the exit. The almost-empty stadium was littered with losing tickets, popcorn and beer cans. Suddenly he stopped, turned around and glanced back at the race track. Owners and jockeys were standing with their family and friends admiring the winning horses. As Ravi spied the billboard, his face lit up and he began to laugh uncontrollably.

"Ha-Ha! It did work. It did happen!" He danced in circles, with raised hands, he was shouting, "Hooray for Number Nine. I knew you wouldn't desert me."

I was scared that he might be losing his mind. His parents back home would blame me because I took him to the races. Urgently, I tried to calm him down. Breathlessly, he uttered, "Look Rajen, Look at the billboard!" As I turned around, I noticed the billboard with the glaring ninth race results.

My eyes scrolled down. Number Two won, Number Four placed, and Number Five showed. I continued down until I saw, with astonishment, what had made Ravi so happy.

Number 9 had come in 9th.

I guess some people find a win in a loss.

# MAGIC PILLS

Frank and his wife had a good marriage except for one thing. Frank was no longer able to "perform" in the bedroom. His wife Emma was a pragmatic woman and ungrudgingly accepted the situation. She repeatedly tried to reassure him that it was only natural for someone of his age. But unfortunately, Frank became obsessed with his inadequacy. He was horrified by the onset of middle age, with its grey hair and slight stomach pouch.

Finally, he confided in his friend and coworker, Tom. This was the man who always had the answers to questions he would be embarrassed to ask anyone else. Tom had the perfect solution.

"Haven't you ever used the little blue pills? They work wonders!"

Frank went to his doctor asking for this miracle cure. The difficulty was not unfamiliar to the doctor, so Frank happily left with a prescription for the amazing pills. Immediately, he and Emma commenced enjoying bedroom bliss.

But things still weren't perfect. Emma was keeping busy in the autumn of her years, and volunteering and visiting their grandchildren often kept her out during the day and exhausted at night. This limited the frequency of their bedroom escapades and Frank soon developed an insatiable need for satisfaction.

Once again, he sought out his coworker, Tom. "I'm having a problem with those blue pills."

Tom was puzzled. "Now what? Don't tell me they didn't work for you."

"No, they work like a charm. But now I...need more...than Emma is up for. She's so preoccupied with everything else in her life."

With an amused expression, Tom replied, "Oh, I see." He thought for a moment. "Hey, Frank? Have you ever noticed how your secretary looks at you? Why not ask Summer to our company's Island Retreat? Since you're one of the top executives, your villa will be isolated from the rest of them. I'll bet that she'll be willing to go and that you'll get completely satisfied."

Frank laughed uncertainly and walked off.

Later that afternoon, he hit send on an email and leaned back in his chair. His mind wandered, and soon he felt that familiar urgency, a hunger that he knew would likely go unattended this evening, and many other evenings. He glanced out of his office door. Summer was standing up near her desk, talking to a client on the phone. She had the phone tucked between her cheek and shoulder and was gesturing with her hands as she spoke. Her skirt swayed as she moved, draping nicely around her hips. Frank started thinking.

He found himself talking to her more and more, complimenting her, noticing when she looked good in a blouse or had her hair pinned up. She did smile at him quite a bit.

*What's the harm?* he thought. *Emma would never find out, and I'd be doing her a favor. I'd stop bothering her so much. And if Summer is interested...*

So gradually, he spent more time thinking about and planning for a pleasurable tryst. As it turned out, the retreat weekend was scheduled for when his wife couldn't accompany him due to a major event in their grandson's school. After gathering up his courage, he finally asked Summer to go with him on the weekend outing.

She blushed and looked pleased. "That sounds wonderful," she said. "Let me make sure it doesn't conflict with anything on my schedule. I'll get back to you tomorrow."

Frank was encouraged by her smiling face. "Sounds good. Let me know."

That evening, Summer sat at a nearby pub with one of her girlfriends.

"This is the boss you have a crush on, right?" Her friend giggled.

"Yeah, but he's married," Summer furrowed her brow and took a sip of wine. "That could get messy. I would feel bad."

"Girl," chided her friend. "Don't pass up this opportunity. Free vacation, time with the big boss with a chance to climb the corporate ladder! You *have* to go!"

The next day Summer told Frank that she would be delighted to join him. Before they left, Tom stopped in his office.

"I can't believe you actually pulled it off, man." He put his fist out to bump Frank's. "You'll have to tell me all about it when you get back."

Frank put on an innocent expression. "I don't know what you are talking about, sir. I am going on a *business* trip with my *secretary*, with whom I have an entirely *platonic relationship*." The two men cracked up.

"Just don't forget to bring plenty of those blue pills with you," reminded Tom. "There isn't a pharmacy on the island."

"Oh I wouldn't forget those pills for the world," Frank reassured him.

It was a beautiful, warm, sunny day when they arrived on the isle. A cool breeze was playing with Summer's bangs, and her eyes sparkled with an excitement. He gazed at her long legs below her shorts, and thought to himself. "Wow! I am the luckiest man on earth with a fantastic weekend ahead of me."

Soon a native couple approached them. The man took his hat off, and in his island accent said, "Welcome to our beautiful island. My name is Jose and this is my wife Elsa. If there's anything you need, please let me know." Jose took the luggage and started loading the Jeep.

Summer began chasing after a peacock, giggling. She was beautiful, but watching her frolic made Ed uncomfortably aware of the age gap between them.

"Your daughter is lovely," Jose's wife commented. Frank frowned and didn't reply.

The villa was at the top of a very steep hill. Just as Tom had said, there were no other buildings surrounding the villa. Slowly, the Jeep climbed the curvy hill and Jose parked it by the building. He brought their luggage inside as Frank and Summer walked around, exploring their weekend home.

"Okay, that should about do it," said Jose. "My wife and I won't be around, but everything you'll need for the weekend is in the refrigerator. There are emergency numbers listed over there by the phone. We'll come back Monday morning to take you to the airport." Frank nodded and smiled, eager for the villa to be theirs alone.

In the front was a gorgeous garden where the aroma of bougainvillea and jasmine filled their lungs. Inside was a large living room, a galley kitchen and an enticing bedroom which were all decorated with a mixture of modern and Island decor. Frank's eyes rested on the wide, luxurious bed. He imagined Summer reclining on those silken sheets. He flushed with anticipation. He could barely wait.

Suddenly, he heard a sweet voice calling, "Frank, join me here and look at this beautiful view." Summer was already on the terrace surveying the majestic Pacific Ocean and its roaring waves. All around there was nothing but white sand, green water and blue skies.

Frank touched her elbow. "Hey, I'm a bit sweaty from the trip," he said. "I'm going to take a quick shower. I'll catch you in a minute, okay?" She gave him a suggestive smile and nodded.

Frank hastily jumped in the shower and was finished in nothing flat! He came out in fresh shorts and a shirt, which he hoped to shed very soon. She was lounging on the couch, gazing out of the huge windows.

"Do you want to shower? I can pour us some drinks. Then we can just..." he paused, looking her up and down, "...relax." Summer stood up and slowly took off her clothes, dropping them piece by piece onto the living room floor. Then she turned and walked to the shower with a sexy swing. Frank

was overwhelmed by her mind-boggling beauty as
he scanned her naked body.

Smiling from ear to ear, he rooted through the
fridge for a bottle of champagne, popped the cork,
and poured two glasses. Then he happily muttered
to himself, "Now it's time for those wonderful
magic pills."

He unzipped the suitcase, flinging clothes
everywhere in search of the container of blue pills.
Instead, in a corner, he found a piece of note paper.
He screamed in disbelief, "What the heck?" He
unfolded the paper, immediately recognizing the
familiar handwriting.

*Oh, my darling, this morning, when you were
showering, I started to put your blood pressure
medicine in the suitcase and found our magic pills.
Silly boy! You thought I'd be going there with you.
Don't worry honey, when you return, the magic
pills and I will be waiting for you.*

# THE HUMANIST

A s soon as we reached our favorite vacation
resort, the kids couldn't wait to rush down to
the beach. It was a month of August. We had just
arrived from hot, steamy Columbus, Ohio to the
refreshingly cool and breezy Bahamas. Sandra took
the kids to enjoy the water, while I took a few
minutes to unwind at the bar overlooking the
ocean.

A bartender fixed me a nice tropical drink. I
lifted the glass to my lips, but before I had even
taken the first sip, the phone behind the bar rang.
The bartender picked it up and spoke a few words,
then turned and indicated that it was a call from the
front desk for me. I took the receiver and heard the
voice of Dipak, my best friend from India. After a
perfunctory hello, his voice choked up, and he
began sobbing. My stomach plunged and my hands
started to shake. What had happened?

Finally, he composed himself and uttered, "Your dad..."

The phone slid out of my hand onto the bar, spilling the drink all over the counter. The color drained from my face. I don't know how long I sat motionless and silent.

"No!" I screamed suddenly, senselessly. "No! No!"

I smashed my forehead on the top of the counter several times. The bartender looked away. How could this happen? Unbelievable. I had just talked to him in the morning before we left Columbus. But now he was gone. My dad, my hero, my god didn't exist anymore. All of a sudden, my shelter had been stripped away.

Someone from the bar ran to the beach to find my wife and kids. They came running to the bar area. I was still sitting in shock. We hugged each other, cried together and walked towards the room hand-in-hand. The phone rang endlessly. My brother from Philadelphia, my sisters from India, my friends and relatives from all over the USA and England were calling. I didn't talk to anyone. I simply couldn't do it. Sandra listened to all the calls, and through her grief, responded accordingly. I sat silently for a long time, and then walked out to the beach.

I found a secluded place where I could stare far away at the horizon. My feet were getting wet from the incoming waves. By now the sunset was over. The sky was still pinkish and the moon was casting its light on the blue water. The ocean was calm as the waves crept onto the shore and then quickly receded. Suddenly, I saw my dad's smiling face on the outgoing waves—his eyes wise and kind, his hair shot through with grey. I tried to grab for him, but ended up with only cold wetness in my hand.

"Where are you going?" I cried out. There was no answer. There was only the sound of the waves lapping on the sand. All I could see was his face on those waves continuing to move further away from me. "Please come back. How am I going to live the rest of my life without you?" No answer came back again.

Many years ago, at age sixteen, I had read Albert Camus' famous novel *Stranger*. Like everyone else, I was fascinated by the first shocking sentences. *Mother died today. Or, maybe, yesterday; I can't be sure...That doesn't mean anything.*

No, no, no. He was wrong. It means everything. There is a huge disparity between Dad "is" and Dad "was." At least in my life, the difference is massive. A major vacuum had suddenly been created.

I sat there for a long time, thinking about him. Night's darkness was starting to enfold me. A cold wind was blowing. I was dressed only in shorts and a T-shirt. My body began to shiver. Someone put a shawl around me, and two hands rested on my shoulder. I turned around. My two sons were standing there in the moonlight.

"Dad, let's go to the room." I got up and slowly walked towards the hotel, resting my hands on their shoulders.

My younger son asked me, "Dad, if you had to describe Grandpa in just two words, what would you say?"

"The Humanist."

"What does that mean?" he questioned.

"A good man." The older son replied. Yes, my father certainly practiced and believed in concern for human dignity and welfare. I endured a totally sleepless night. Sandra kept trying to console me. Finally, I ran out of tears.

The next day, I took an early flight to Miami, with a connecting flight to London. I met my brother, Bharat, on a flight to Bombay. Throughout that ten hour flight, I was either crying or sadly looking at the sky outside the cabin's window. Bharat was calmly talking about the next steps we would have to take upon our arrival in India. These involved handling Dad's affairs and convincing Mom to return with us to the United States. I just nodded my head and asked him to make all those decisions.

At the airport, my friend Dipak and Bharat's brother in-law came to pick us up. I cried on Dipak's shoulder. He was like a third son to my dad. Bharat and I sat on the back seat.

Dipak started the car, then turned around and looked at me and said quietly, "Your mom was sitting exactly where Bharat is now. Your dad sat next to her in the spot where you are sitting. Even before I could start the engine, he had a massive heart attack and fell in your mom's lap." All at once, my mind drifted back to a few years ago when my father had told me that one day he would love to go quickly. No ambulance, no hospital visits, no IV or oxygen. His wish had ultimately been granted, although it was a small comfort.

Going through the funeral process was very painful. Hundreds of people showed up to pay their respect to him. Attendees included both rich and poor, educated and uneducated. He was a very beloved and respected person in the community. Among the visitors, I noticed that one fruit vendor was crying hysterically. I remembered that dad always bought fresh bananas from him.

One of dad's Muslim friends, Mr. Ali, pulled me aside and, in a sad voice, told me a story about Dad.

"Your dad was a secular man. Back in 1946, all of us Hindus and Muslims fought against Britishers under the Congress party. One time Britishers had an arrest warrant on me. I was looking for a hideout place.

"So your Dad gave me an idea, 'If you hide in a Hindu's home, they will never look for you there.'

"I told him, 'I agree, but no Hindu will keep a Muslim in his home.'"

Ali paused and wiped his tears. "Your dad kept me in his home for thirty days. I have no doubt he saved my life." Then he laughed a little. "After I left, your Brahmin grandma had to sprinkle holy Ganges water all over the house to make it sacred again."

Later, one of the prominent judges stopped me and told me, "Your dad was a principled man. He was strongly against discrimination. Not only against discrimination toward minorities but against anyone, even those who were considered to be in the majority. When he visited the USA in 1978, he followed a landmark Supreme Court 'reverse discrimination' case, Regents of University of California versus Alan Bakke. He was fascinated with that result, and when he came back he cited Bakke case results in arguments for one reverse discrimination case in the education field."

One early morning a few days after the funeral, my younger sister Uma and I were sitting on the front porch swings having tea. A woman with high cheekbones and a white sari was walking down the sidewalk toward the house. As she got closer, she looked over at us and paused. "Namaste," she said quietly. Then she opened the gate and came in, walking straight to the rose bushes in front of the house. After bowing for a few minutes, she whispered some prayers, wiped her tears and left.

"Who is that woman?" wondered Uma after she was gone. "Do you know her?"

I nodded. "This is an interesting story about Dad. Last January when I was visiting, he and I were sitting right here one morning. I saw that same woman approaching our house. Dad got up, cut some beautiful roses and made a nice bouquet for her. She thanked him and left. I saw her walking towards the temple across the street, so I jokingly asked him, 'Hey Dad, do you know where those flowers are going? That lady is walking to the temple. Inside the temple there are a few statues of a god. She is going to worship and leave those flowers at the feet of her god. Isn't it funny that a nonbeliever like you is giving her flowers to bring to the temple?'

Very calmly and with a smile, he answered, 'I know where she's taking those flowers and what she will be doing inside that temple. But I am a humanist. My mission is to make another human happy, which I did. After I give her flowers, they become her flowers. Whether she takes them to a temple or a funeral home is between her and her soul. I have fulfilled my goal to make another human happy."

Uma said, "Wow, I didn't know that story."

I thought for a while and came up with an idea. "You know, Uma, I bet we all know some stories about him which others in the family don't know happened. Why don't we talk about relating our special stories to each other? And, of course, I bet Mom must know many, also."

That afternoon we all sat in the living room for afternoon tea. I asked mom, "Can you tell us something about Dad which we kids don't know?" Mom thought for a while and said, "Did you see that banana vendor crying for so long at the funeral? Your dad had arranged a scholarship for his son to continue his education."

"We all know that, Mom." Bharat interrupted. "Dad was deeply disturbed by the fact that after high school, many poor kids in India couldn't afford to go to college. So he formed a group made out of financially well-to-do lawyers, doctors and businessmen. Then he would present applicable students to them. Everyone would pledge some money for student's tuition and miscellaneous expenses."

"I remember," Uma interjected. "But the condition was that the candidate must pass high school with all As or O's (Outstanding)."

"That's right," Mom said, "However, what you don't know is how this boy, Ramesh got the scholarship. He received a C on his final exam. Your dad was worried that he would not be eligible for the scholarship. That night he kept constantly pacing around the house and garden. Finally, I asked him what was the problem, and this is what he told me. 'I really like this boy. Ramesh is a smart young man and would do fine in college. Unfortunately, the day before the final exam, his father was hospitalized and Ramesh spent the entire night with him in the hospital. We visited that evening and there he was, reading a school textbook. Obviously, he would not have been in a good frame of mind to take a final exam the following day. But my friends are not going to give him a pass. They always follow the requirements of giving a scholarship without any exceptions. I really like this student. Ramesh should go to college, or otherwise, he will work for his dad or not attain his potential in a factory job. His knowledge and understanding have always impressed me.'"

Mom paused for a while and my elder sister Jaya got her a glass of water. After a few sips, she continued, "Your dad couldn't sleep that night, worrying about that boy. He told me there was only one way to resolve the issue. He had all of the applicants' marksheets in his briefcase. If he could change the boy's grades from C to O, he would be qualified for the scholarship. However, it was against his principles. He mentioned to me, 'I taught our kids not to lie or cheat. All my life I have preached not to do anything unlawful or irregular. So how can I do this?'

"Then he looked at me and jokingly said, 'What would your god say about this?' I thought for a minute and told him, 'You know that I am a religious person and my God also tells me not to lie or cheat. However, the same religion says that when someone's life is in danger then it's OK to lie. Marium, our Christian neighbor, told me one day that the Bible says the same thing.'

"To that your dad replied, 'I agree. It's OK to lie to save someone's life. So then the question is, what do we have here? Is it a life or death situation? In a way it is. This child's future and that of his next generation is at stake. If he goes to college and becomes a doctor or an engineer, his life will be totally different.'

"We both struggled that night to make the right decision. The next morning, the marksheet was lying on the dining table showing O grades."

Her story finished, Mom got up and took the teapot and glasses into the kitchen. I turned to my siblings. "What do you think? Who changed the mark sheet? A true religious person like mom, or a nonbeliever like dad? One of them crossed the boundary that night."

My brother and I agreed, "I bet Dad did it."

"No, it must be Mom," said the sisters.

Mom came back in from the kitchen to collect the last few dishes. "Mom!" we all begged. "Would you please tell us who changed that marksheet?"

She smiled serenely. "Does it matter?" she asked. "We both dreamed of the same ideal world." Then she turned and walked back into the kitchen.

# PIZZA PARTY

Doctor Munjal's family made a yearly trip to India to visit his extended family and old friends. This year, his wife, Ketki, had a rather unusual plan.

"Are you listening to me?" Ketki was gathering items for their trip, chattering away to her husband, who was watching a televised golf match.

"I've decided that while we are there, we're going to host a pizza party in the village," she declared. "We'll invite all of your friends and your family's friends. We'll serve homemade pizzas. We'll give them a taste of America! I am going to collect most of the ingredients here in the states and bring them over with us. Isn't that a great idea? We'll have so much fun."

Dr. Munjal, only half-listening to her, and not wanting to get into an argument, just nodded his head. Their ten-year-old daughter, Nilu, who had been sitting nearby, jumped from her chair with excitement.

"Let's do it, Mom. That would be awesome! I'm sure everyone would love some real American pizza."

Over the next few weeks, Ketki made a big list and shopped for all the ingredients which she would be able to take with her. Finally, with a few extra suitcases, the family reached a small town in India. After resting a few days to recover from jet lag, Ketki asked Munjal to send invitations for the pizza party to be held the following Sunday.

On Saturday afternoon, she pulled out and organized the ingredients. "Oh, no!" she said to herself. She realized that she was missing an important item. For some reason, she had neglected to obtain any mushrooms.

"Do you think we can do without them?" wondered Ketki doubtfully.

"No, Mom! Everyone knows that pizza has mushrooms!" Nilu shrieked.

With some quick thinking, Ketki got an idea. Turning to the household's maid, she gave some instructions. "I'd like you to go out to the *vadi* and pick some mushrooms. There are plenty in the creek bed."

"Don't have her do that!" Munjal shouted urgently from the other room, "Some wild mushrooms are poisonous."

"No, sir, it is okay," assured the maid. "I often see critters eating them and nothing bad happens."

Just to be extra careful, Ketki decided to collect them herself. She took a large basket and filled it with the wild mushrooms. When the basket was full, she returned to the house and proceeded to thoroughly wash, and slice them for the big pizza dinner.

As she was slicing, there was a knock at the door.

"Hello," said a sturdy woman with a little girl and a dog in tow. "I am Radha. We spoke on the phone. You hired me to help serve at your event tonight?"

"Oh, hello," said Ketki. "I'm so happy you're here. What about them?"

"I am sorry, I had nowhere to take them while I work," she explained. "Is it okay if they stay here? They're both very good. Her name is Ramli and his name is Motio."

Ketki suddenly got an idea. "Yes, of course, you can put him on the back porch and she can stay in here with you and help with the food. Come, help me prepare these ingredients."

A few moments later, Ketki slipped out to the back porch with a double handful of the mushrooms. The dog sloppily ate every one of them. *If the dog gets sick, I'll know they were dangerous.* Dishonest and unkind, perhaps, but if the dog died, she would be sure to compensate the woman.

All morning long, Ketki watched Motio, and the wild mushrooms didn't seem to affect him, so she decided to use them on the pizzas. However, she also thought that someone should keep an eye on the dog. Once the event started, Ketki instructed Ramli to watch the dog and tell her immediately if it anything bad happened to him.

The meal was a great success, everyone loved being able to sample a genuine American pizza. Radha even had served them wearing a white apron and chef's cap.

After everyone had finished eating, the guests relaxed, socialized, and started to play cards when Radha's daughter came in running. She rushed up to Ketki and whispered something in her ear. "Mrs.

Patel, Motio is dead!" Radha, who was standing
next to Ketki, started to cry and hurried out to find
her beloved dog.

Ketki went into hysterics. Her husband came
into the kitchen and tried to calm her down. With
tears in her eyes, she told him what had happened.
"I've made a terrible mistake. I used those field
mushrooms on the pizzas. Radha's dog ate some
and now he has died!"

He immediately pulled his buddy Pranav, a local
Indian doctor, to one side and informed him about
the situation. "I'm an optometrist," said Dr. Munjal,
"I have no idea how to treat poisoning! I need your
help here." Although he couldn't believe what had
been done, Doctor Pranav assessed the situation
and made a decision.

"This isn't good, but I think it can be taken care
of swiftly," he said firmly. "I'll call for an ambulance
and when the medical personnel arrive we'll give
everyone enemas and also pump out their stomach.
Everything will be fine. Just keep them calm."

Ketki began to cry from embarrassment.
"Stomach pumps and enemas? How horrid!"

Dr. Pranav went out to tell the crowd that there
was a problem. The guests were soon buzzing with
apprehension. Soon, they could hear the siren as
the ambulance came down the road. The EMTs and
the doctor brought in their medical bags and all the
necessary equipment to carry out the tasks before
them.

One by one, they took the guests into the house's
two bathrooms. They gave each person an enema
and pumped out their stomach. Everyone was
frightened and humiliated at the uncomfortable
experience.

All the party guests were looking quite weak as
they sat around the living room. Once the last

person was attended to, an EMT came out and reassured the group.

"I know that wasn't pleasant, but you are all going to be okay. Eat mild foods this evening. If anyone experiences any symptoms of toxicity—convulsions, fever, difficulty breathing—go to the hospital right away."

The guests were muttering to one another. "What kind of parties do these Americans throw? First they feed you and then they empty everything out."

Ketki and Munjal sent the guests on their way, apologizing and thanking them for attending.

Exhausted and ashamed, Ketki slunk into the kitchen and began washing dishes. The hired server came into the kitchen, wiping her eyes.

"Oh, Radha." Ketki dried her hands. "I am so sorry about all of this. Here is ten thousand rupees, for your dog."

Radha sniffed. Then she calmly took the money, put it inside her blouse, and said, "You know, Ma'am, you foreigners are very generous. That SOB car driver who ran over my poor little dog didn't even stop!

# FOURTH DOWN AND INCHES

*Friday, 26 September 2008–Mozart Cafe*

Susanna watched through a front window as her husband Troy approached the Mozart Cafe's entrance. After ten years of marriage and three daughters, she could tell his frame of mind by just looking at him. She knew from his slouched gait that today had not been a good day for him. Being a well-built, muscular man, he usually had a very confident walk. As he came through the door, she rose from her chair, and waved at him with a big smile on her face. He acknowledged Susanna's wave and came toward her table. She could hear the cafe's piano player pounding out some ragtime tunes, but the look on Troy's face held no mirth. She greeted him with a kiss on the cheek and decided to figure out what was wrong. Susanna waited for him to slide into the big booth and settle himself. After Troy had taken a sip of water and released a big sigh, Susanna took a deep breath and began.

"So, what's new?" she asked.

Troy's shoulders slumped. "You remember Mark from the main office? Well, he visited our branch today. We talked about my sales numbers. If I can't get two more closings done, or at least *scheduled* by the end of the month, the company and I will be parting ways."

"Troy!" exclaimed Susanna, squeezing his shoulder. "Honey, I am so sorry. That is terrible!"

He reached up and grabbed her hand. "He talked to me and a few other people. I will try my hardest, but it's been so tough since the crash last October. The economy's tanked, no one wants to buy or sell. Everyone is all clenched up. I don't know how I'm ever going to make that deadline." He sighed and raked his hands through his hair. "Although, I have one contract ready, with the closing scheduled for Monday, I don't have any prospects for the near future. Since Tuesday is the thirtieth, and thereby the last day of this month, I don't see any opportunity for a closing or a new contract in four days." Troy ticked off the days on his fingers. "We might as well realize that I'll probably be joining the unemployed." He gave a discouraged frown and began looking at the menu.

Susanna felt panic welling up. She kept a neutral, loving expression on her face so she wouldn't make Troy feel even worse. She took a breath and looked around cheerlessly, as people were starting to come in to the cafe for Friday night's happy hour. The music was still upbeat, but now she had a knot in the pit of her stomach, and the music was only an annoyance. She grabbed a menu andstared at it without really seeing it. Troy ordered his favorite beer and was getting ready to look at the specials, but the menu's words became a simple blur to Susanna.

Troy looked at his wife, but she was gazing at the paintings of far-away places like Saltzburg and Vienna, which was the motif of the cafe. *What are we going to do?* she wondered. *We'll have to sell the house and move in with Mom. That will move us into a different school district right in the middle of Lisa and Natalie's school year! Could I even find a job if I had to go back to work full time?*

Her head was throbbing and her stomach began churning. The music had turned to a fast-paced Cole Porter number. That sound, coupled with the loud voices of happy people and clanking dishes suddenly made her hot and dizzy. At that moment, the waiter appeared.

"Honey, order whatever you want," Troy encouraged.

But she was still stunned by his revelation. Her mouth was dry. "I'm feeling a bit queasy; I'll just have some tea for now."

Troy raised his eyebrows. Either he didn't grasp the tumult in her head, or he couldn't acknowledge his own overwhelming fears.

*Saturday, 27 September 2008–Mr. and Mrs. Smith and the neighborhood tour*
"We want to go back and look at the neighborhood one last time. You understand. Just so we're completely certain." Mr. Smith's voice on the phone sounded apologetic but firm.

"It's not unusual for buyers to want one last look at a house before their closing date," reassured Troy. "It isn't an inconvenience at all. Let's schedule it." Troy was delighted to assist his future buyers.

"Will you meet me at the office or should I pick you up?"

"No. Since there's no issue, my wife and I would like to tour the neighborhood by ourselves. Lola is very cautious and gets anxious over small details. She wants to make sure there's no mistake in her choice of a house and neighborhood. Right now, she'd like to learn more about the neighbors. Me—I don't care so much. But after my divorce, I have learned my lesson. A happy wife makes for a happy life." He laughed.

"Ok. Enjoy canvassing the neighborhood. It's a lovely day for such an excursion. Don't forget to visit the Acropolis for a great Mediterranean lunch. I'll talk to you later in the afternoon." On that lighthearted note, Troy hung up the phone.

About four thirty, Mr. Smith called Troy and gave him some pleasant news concerning their earlier outing. "Well, we were able to meet some of the neighbors. The family across the street has teenagers who seemed quite respectful. Everyone that we met around the cul- de-sac was nice. We visited with the older couple on the north side. Unfortunately, the woman who lives in the house on the other side wasn't home. Yet, the older couple said they knew her and that she was always friendly and personable."

"That's great," said Troy, with a private sigh of relief. At least he would be leaving the company with one final sale under his belt. Maybe enough for a good reference? "I'll see you on Monday morning to sign all the necessary papers at the closing. Then, the house will be yours officially." After the phone conversation ended, a new thought crossed Troy's mind. *I wish this had been a two-fer. If I had been involved in selling his home in Columbus and then sold the Clintonville cottage to him and the lovely*

*new trophy wife, I could have been paid on both
ends of the deal. I wish they were all two-fers, then
my numbers would be looking good. They would
have definitely kept me out of the unemployment
office.*

*Sunday, 28 September 2008–A day with kids*

This Sunday was very different for Troy and
Susanna's family. Normally, Troy was up early and
worked hard all day on open houses and showings.
Instead, Troy grimly made breakfast for the kids.
They did not understand the implications of his
unusual presence and were thrilled to have Dad
home with them. Troy tried to enjoy the day off and
the precious time with his children, but the future
hung over him like a dark cloud. After the kids got
out of the pool, and they had enjoyed a delicious
barbecue, Troy gently told them about the situation
with the housing market and how his job was being
affected by it. As calmly as possible, he described
the possibility of a smaller house and the chance of
spending some time living at grandma's home. The
older girl was quiet, and the youngest didn't really
follow the conversation, but his middle child,
Natalie, jumped in to voice her disapproval.

"I'll have to sleep with Grandma? No way, she
snores and I won't be able to sleep."

They all had a laugh and Troy assured her that
sleeping with Grandma would only be a temporary
solution if it were ever needed.

*Monday, 29 September 2008–Closing and
Monday Night Football*

Troy was hustling all day trying to get the last
scheduled closing done with the Smiths. Everything
had gone as planned with no unexpected snags.
Even though the closing had been successful, there
were no more prospects to prevent his dismissal the

following day. He looked lost when he came in the door that night. Susanna braced herself for what seemed like the inevitable. The family ate dinner together, and once the children were off to bed, the couple sat at the kitchen table together with cups of coffee.

Troy rubbed his forehead and groaned. "The facts are, the unemployment rate is hovering around 7.2 percent, the mortgage interest rate is 5.89 percent, and the housing market is down 18 percent. Today the stock market plunged seven percent! Who would buy a house in this environment? Even though it's a very attractive buyer's market, there's too much uncertainty in our economy. Buying a house is a long term commitment. It's going to be some time before buyers have enough confidence and are willing to start buying again."

"I know things look grim," Susanna said softly, "but don't declare defeat yet."

Troy leaned on his hand and sipped coffee despondently. "The fact is, this night will pass and the sun will rise in the morning. If can't pull off a miracle and somehow get one more commitment tomorrow, I'll be without a job."

"Don't be pessimistic, honey," she encouraged. "Something could still happen. You have one more day."

"Damn it, Sue," Troy snapped. "That's realism, not pessimism. I see the world as it is." He stood up, abandoning his coffee, and stomped into the bedroom.

She rolled her eyes in exasperation. She thought of the young, hot-shot realtor she had married, and all the ambition he had possessed. Since the national housing crisis had hit, there was a defeated, frightened edge to him that wasn't there before. Susanna knew better then to argue further when he was like this. She climbed into bed next to him, turned over and wiped her tears and quietly said, "Good night."

They both tried to sleep, but it eluded them. They tossed and turned for half an hour. Susanna's mind wandered to more pleasant things.

Suddenly, she sat up in bed. "Troy, we're missing the Giants versus the Cowboys! Monday Night Football!" Troy never missed watching one of those games, and today his favorite team, the Giants, was scheduled to play.

Troy leapt out of the bed. "Good grief, I completely forgot! It's the final game of the season. Let's give our minds something else to think about tonight. We can catch the tail end of the game if we hurry!"

So they rushed downstairs to the family room. Troy quickly turned on the TV. The Giants were down by two points and now had possession of the ball. Only one minute remained left on the clock. The ball was on the thirty-six yard line. Earlier in the game, mentioned the commentator, their kicker had missed a field goal from that distance. If the Giants could move the ball a few inches for a first down, they would get three more tries to move the ball closer to the goal. This would give the kicker a much better chance. With the three points for a field goal, the Giants would win the game and qualify for the playoffs. Troy's heart started to pound, as he nervously rooted for his team.

Susanna, being her generally optimistic self, tried to make peace after the earlier argument. "Don't worry, they'll make it."

Troy just sighed and thought *this game is just like my life. It all comes down to fourth and inches. One more contract and we will be fine. If not, my life is going to be very different, and not for the better.*

On the next play, the Giants moved the ball to the thirty yard line. When their remaining timeouts had been used, the kicker perfectly scored the winning field goal.

*Tuesday, 30 September 2008—Mr. Smith's early morning phone call*

Susanna let Troy sleep knowing that he had stayed up until the early morning, and there was no work waiting at the office. Finally, he was awakened by the sound of his ringing phone. Puzzled, he saw Mr. Smith's number.

"Hello, Jack."

"Hi, good morning, Troy."

"What can I help you with this morning?"

"Well, we can't move into this house," said Mr. Smith. Troy's stomach churned.

"What? What's wrong with the house? Did the inspector miss anything?"

"Oh, no. Nothing is actually wrong with the house itself."

"Then what? You closed on the house yesterday with no issues. The money is already dispersed from your account to the seller's account. It's a done deal, my friend. There's no way you can backtrack."

"I understand. But here's the problem ..." After a long pause, Mr. Smith sighed and continued.

"It's kind of awkward. It turns out that our next door neighbor is my ex-wife. *She's* the so-called 'personable neighbor' that the older couple told us about. What would they know? My sweet Lola is hysterical! We're still at the hotel. She is not going to move into that house. I need to fix this or my marriage is over. Troy, my friend, I understand that

I purchased this house and there is no going back now. I need you to put this on the market right away. I need to sell it and I want you to do it. And please put in a bid on that other house we liked in Westerville."

Troy's heart pounded, but he tried to keep his voice steady on the phone. "Oh, Jack. I'm so sorry about this messy situation, but I'll get to work right away to help you purchase the other house. I'm positive it hasn't already sold. As soon as I verify that it's still for sale, I'll start the listing process for yesterday's purchase."

As he hung up, a broad smile spread across Troy's face. He couldn't believe it. This was the legendary "twofer". He had sold the house, and now he was selling it again. *I got my second contract on the same house within twenty-four hours.*

"Susanna!" he boomed, running to the kitchen. He found her preparing lunches for the girls. She had paused with a peanut butter knife aloft in her hand and was watching him with a worried expression. "Susanna, you are not going to believe this one." He picked up the youngest daughter and danced around with her on his shoulders, exuberantly singing "I got a twofer...a twofer!" He told his wife what had just happened. Her face lit up more and more as the story unfolded.

"What does that mean, Daddy?" asked Natalie.

"It means we're going to be fine, honey," Troy squeezed her and smiled. "It means we can stay here."

Susanna thought for a minute and said, "You're wrong, Troy."

His head snapped up. "What do you mean?"

"Actually you didn't get a twofer, you got a threefer. You managed to get three contracts from one client. The buy, the resale, and the third place in Westerville! Thank goodness for Mr. Smith's divorce!"

Troy considered what Susanna had just said. "You're right. My, aren't you the smart one. I did get a threefer. I can't wait to tell my boss."

Then he walked over to her and the girls, giving them all hugs and kisses. "Just like I got this threefer with you!"

# Acknowledgements

No creative endeavor can come to fruition without inspiration and support, so I want to thank my family and friends. A very special thanks to my writing coach and mentor, Jen Knox, and my phenomenal editor, Rebecca Grubb. I want to thank Karen Phillips for creating a stunning book cover, and Meredith Bond for the great-looking formatting. Thank you to the Eastside Writers Group: Charles O'Donnell, Jodi Rath, and the rest of the writers for critiquing and providing positive feedback. Thank you, M. C. Smith for pre-editing the stories and pushing me to the finish line.R.K. Story and my South Carolina friends deserve special thanks for the many years spent listening to my tales. How can I forget my friends in Wine Meetup Group? Friday night wine made me relaxed and inspired me to write more stories on Saturday. My Tuesday night philosophy group always provided a conceptual core for my plots.

And finally, special gratitude to the late Gujarati writers Rajendra Dave and Harnish Jani for believing in my work.

# ABOUT THE AUTHOR

 Upen Dave was born and raised in India. He came to the USA in the early seventies and acquired a Master of Structural Engineering at George Washington University. He recently retired from a long career in a nuclear engineering. Although an engineer by profession, he had an intense interest in literature that began in childhood. His first story, "Sun Rise," was published in the Gujarati magazine *Shadhana* when Upen was fifteen. Additional stories were published in New Jersey and Chicago magazines in the Gujarati language. An avid reader from youth, he is influenced by his favorite authors O. Henry, Ernest Hemingway, and Jean Paul Sartre. He writes short stories set in both the US and around the world—but always with a subtle ending. The stories in this book not only contain the unexpected surprises, but are often bittersweet. He has been able to capture the human spirit and all life's twists and turns. Some of these stories are based on his personal history, people whom he has encountered and situations which he has faced. Upen's humor is evidenced in each story—some with extreme hilarity and others with a subtle charm. It's a unique collection and will be rewarding to everyone who reads it. These stories capture the irony of life.

Made in the USA
Monee, IL
17 March 2022